Alexandra's Riddle

A NORTHWEST MAGIC NOVEL

Alexandra's Riddle

ELISA KEYSTON

Crimson Fox
PUBLISHING

TURNER, OREGON

Chapter 1

Cass frowned, shielding her eyes against the glare of the late-summer sun as she peered up at the house before her. The looming Queen Anne Victorian looked more weathered than it had the last time she'd seen it—the siding was peeling, and the vibrant lavender-and-white paint she remembered so vividly from her childhood had faded to a dull gray—but it still looked majestic, standing there nestled between firs and pines and oaks so ancient that their trunks were too massive for a person to get their arms around.

She sighed, running her fingers through her perpetually-tangled hair. It wasn't a bad house, really. Despite the paint and the thick blanket of needles and moss on the roof, the home had been well maintained. Nothing a little T.L.C. couldn't take care of.

No, the biggest problem—for Cass, at least—was that the house was immense. Far too large for one person to have to deal with. The main part of the house was three stories tall if you counted the finished attic; and, of course, there was also the turret with its observatory and the glass-walled solarium on the south end of the house. How Aunt Alexandra had managed to maintain a home of this magnitude, Cass had no idea.

Under her breath, she muttered, "I didn't sign up for this." Then she pulled the keys that her great-aunt's attorney had given her out of her jeans pocket and moved to unlock the front door.

As she stood there jiggling the keys in the lock, struggling to force the stiff deadbolt to turn, a familiar sensation prickled across her skin, leaving a wave of gooseflesh in its wake. That ominous, crawling feeling in the pit of her stomach that she knew all too well. She paused, staring at the keys in her hand without really seeing them. "Now what?" she murmured.

As if in response, a cheery voice from behind her called, "Yoo-hoo! Are you Cassandra?"

Cass turned her head to see a middle-aged woman with a perky blonde perm about twenty-five years out of style waving exuberantly. *Not exactly your typical harbinger of doom,* Cass thought wryly. But then again, her premonitory feelings had never exactly been predictable—as contradictory as that seemed.

"Uh, it's Cass," she corrected as the woman bustled across the overgrown yard and up the steps onto the porch. "But yeah."

"Wonderful. We've been expecting you. My name's Connie Fischer, I live across the street." She stuck out her hand expectantly. Cass stared at her for a minute, her own hands full of doorknob and keys; but when Connie didn't seem to get the message, Cass gave up on the lock and reached to shake her hand.

Connie had jewel-encrusted rings on every finger. They scraped across Cass's palm, and the charms on her bracelet jangled as she pumped Cass's arm up and down with just as much intensity as you'd expect from a *Connie* with hair that pert. Cass had never been much of a jewelry-wearer, apart from a small, old-fashioned skeleton key on a tarnished silver chain that she wore around her neck. That had been a gift from Aunt Alexandra, years ago. Alexandra had worn even more jewelry than Connie—long-chained necklaces, bangles, huge hoop earrings so heavy that they'd stretched her earlobes practically to her shoulders. Once, when Cass was visiting as a little girl, she'd come across the key in Alexandra's jewelry box while playing dress-up. It was so different from any of the other pieces her great-aunt owned, so simple in comparison to her ornate jewels; but Cass had thought it was brimming with adventure and mystery. She'd longed to explore every corner of the old Victorian house until she found the door that the key unlocked.

Alexandra had been so amused by Cass's devotion to the plain key necklace that she'd told Cass she could keep it. Cass had worn it ever since, even though she knew logically that it was probably just the key to an old china cabinet or maybe a dusty chest of linens.

She felt a pang now at the memory. Even into her nineties,

Alexandra had had so much *life* in her. It still felt impossible that she could be gone.

"Your aunt was so beloved here in Riddle, Cassandra," Connie said, as if she'd read Cass's mind. "She kept to herself, but she was so sweet... given the opportunity. She'll be sorely missed." She brushed her hands off on her khaki pants, charm bracelet tinkling. "But now you're here, and I'm so glad. Will you and your husband be moving into Alexandra's home?"

Cass sighed, turning back to the jammed deadbolt and bracing herself for this all-too-familiar turn in the conversation. "I'm not married, actually."

"Oh?" Connie's voice had a loaded tone to it, one Cass had heard many times before—especially since she'd turned thirty. She could almost *feel* the wheels in Connie's head turning, wondering what was "wrong" with her. Divorced? Antisocial? The product of overbearing parents who chased away any eligible bachelor with a shotgun?

She wasn't any of those things (well, maybe the antisocial part), but the truth wasn't exactly something easily explained... or believed. It was easier to let people think what they wanted than even waste her breath on the truth.

"Well, Riddle's a small town, Cassandra," Connie went on at last. "There aren't too many eligible bachelors around here. That are your age, anyway. People tend to marry a bit younger around here. I suppose there's always Roseburg..."

"I'm not looking," Cass broke in, teeth clenched.

"Oh," Connie said again, a different tone in her voice now. "Well, never mind. Alexandra was a spinster, too. What matters is that you're here now. And I do hope you'll be planning on staying."

"Actually," Cass said, shoving her hip against the door and twisting the key as hard as she could, "I was only planning on sticking around long enough to get all of Aunt Alexandra's stuff sorted. Probably just a few months."

Connie's brown eyebrows knitted over her green eyes. "That's all? I heard you got a job over at the library."

Cass snorted. It really was true, what they said about news traveling fast in a small town. "Well, yeah," she said. "A girl's gotta eat. And, you know, pay down her crippling student loans. An MLIS doesn't come for free."

"Oh, of course." Connie's face fell, and Cass quirked an eyebrow. Connie seemed a good deal more disappointed than she should have been for someone who'd never met Cass before. She really should have had no interest in where Cass lived or for how long.

"It's just that..." Connie trailed off, seeming to notice for the first time that Cass was having a hard time getting the door open. "Oh, you need to pull it toward you, dear. Like this." She pushed Cass aside and yanked the door handle firmly. There was the scraping of metal and then the lock turned. When Cass stared, she shrugged. "I've been coming over here to feed Onyx since

Alexandra passed."

Oh. Right. The cat. Cass suppressed the urge to heave a sigh. That was another bother. Cass liked cats, but the thing about pets was that they had a way of tying you down. She didn't want to be one of those jerks who dumped her animals off at a shelter every time she was ready to move on. Better to not acquire them in the first place. She wondered if Connie would be willing to take Onyx when the time came.

The door opened, and Cass stepped through it. The inside of the house smelled nostalgic, a homey combination of basil and old wood. Cass looked around the high-ceilinged entry hall, with its ancient silk wallpaper, the ornate pattern faded with age. A coat rack stood next to the front door, adorned with old-fashioned, long dress coats in rich burgundies and olive greens. Very Alexandra.

"Do you need help carrying anything from your car, Cassandra?" Connie's footsteps echoed off the woodblock as she followed Cass into the house.

"It's Cass. No, I just have a few suitcases, nothing major. I can manage."

"No furniture?"

Cass laughed in exasperation, her tolerance for this busybody reaching its limit. "Why would I bring furniture? I've got a whole house full of it now."

Connie's smile faltered, and Cass felt a slight twinge of guilt. Maybe she did need to work on that whole antisocial thing.

"Of course," said Connie. "Well, listen. I wanted to ask you one more thing, while we were in a more, you know, private setting." Her words made the ominous feeling start crawling through Cass's stomach again. "Have you gotten any offers for the house yet?"

That wasn't what Cass had been expecting. She didn't know *what* she'd been expecting, honestly, but that wasn't it.

"Uh, no," she answered. "I just got here. I have to thin stuff out before I can think about listing it."

Connie nodded. "Well, when the time comes, I hope you'll keep the good of the community in mind."

Cass blinked. "What's that supposed to mean?"

"It's nothing to alarm you. You'll get a better sense of my meaning the longer you're here. But your great-aunt loved this house, Cassandra. She loved Riddle. I hope you'll keep that in mind."

Cass felt completely lost at that point. "Mrs. Fischer, what are you even talking about?" she asked.

"Never mind, never mind. You've got a busy day ahead of you, unpacking and everything. I'll let you get to it. There's food for Onyx in the kitchen. And don't forget that the plants in the solarium will need watering. Feel free to drop by if you need anything. I'm just across the street."

"Wait, Mrs. Fischer—"

But as quickly as she'd come, Connie bustled out the door and down the front drive. Cass stared after her retreating form. What had that been about?

"Leave it to Aunt Alexandra to settle down in a town full of fruitcakes," she grumbled under her breath.

As she moved to shut the front door, a glint of sunlight reflected two green pinpricks in the corner. Cass narrowed her eyes. "Onyx? Kitty, kitty?"

The creature stirred and Cass groaned. Definitely not a cat. So the premonition she'd had earlier hadn't been because of Connie after all.

"Just what I needed," she said. "You'd think Aunt Alexandra would have done something to keep you guys out." She grabbed a dusty umbrella out of the tall urn next to the coat rack and brandished it at the creature, shooing it toward the door.

A small, almost human-like being, with bronze skin the color of autumn oak leaves, dashed out of the corner. A brownie. It ducked and jabbered at Cass in the sharp, guttural language she'd come to recognize over the years, even if she didn't understand what any of the words meant. It sounded like a cross between squirrel chatter and the caw of a crow—some unfamiliar birdsong that those without Sight could dismiss as normal, mundane, even if they couldn't place what animal was making it.

Cass knew better. She'd been Seeing for far too long to trust anything unfamiliar in the forest.

"Yeah, yeah. I don't want to hear it," she said, prodding the brownie along with the umbrella. "Get out and stay out."

She slammed the door and cursed in annoyance. Then she stormed through the maze of rooms toward the back of the house, where she remembered the kitchen being located. After banging her way through half a dozen cluttered cupboards, she found what she was looking for.

The brownie was sitting among the fronds of a large, curling fern when Cass opened the front door again. It glared at her as she produced the metal colander and pointedly set it in the center of the top step. "That'll fix you," she said with a smirk. The brownie watched, scowling, as the purple door slammed. Then it slunk into the ferns.

Cass leaned against the closed door, looking up at the pendant lamp with its Tiffany shade suspended from the entryway's high ceiling. She'd been here all of ten minutes, and already she'd been inundated with nosy neighbors and a pest infestation of the magical variety. She didn't even want to know what was waiting for her on the second floor, let alone the rest of this behemoth house.

"Welcome to Riddle, Cass," she said aloud, hearing the way her voice echoed off the cavernous ceiling and trying to ignore the premonitory goosebumps rippling across her skin. "Looks like you're in for a fun time."

Chapter 2

"You know, some people would *like* to have brownies around," Cass's friend Emma said. Her voice sounded tinny over the speakerphone, which was propped on top of a stack of boxes on the other side of the room. "They're handy. I heard that if you leave them food, they'll do chores around the house for you. If you hadn't chased that one off, it would probably be helping you right now with... whatever it is you're doing."

What Cass was doing was sitting in the middle of the floor in one of Aunt Alexandra's seemingly endless book rooms, sorting through the dusty volumes that had been stacked haphazardly on the shelves. "I'd rather do it myself, thanks," she said. "You forget, Em, I've seen these things. They have no concept of personal hygiene. The last thing I want is their grubby little hands washing my dishes or something."

"It's so unfair," said Emma, the faintest hint of a whine in her voice, "that you get to see these things and you don't even care, while I'm sitting here dying for one genuine paranormal sighting and I get zilch."

Cass scrunched her nose, pulling a dusty volume out of the stack and squinting to read the faded title on its spine. *Soldiers of the Great War, Volume Three*. There was no sign of volumes one or two anywhere in the room. She shook her head and tossed the book onto the giveaway pile. "Does it not occur to you that maybe if you *could* see the 'paranormal', you might not be as interested?"

Emma gasped in horror. Perish the thought. After all, her profession was officially listed on her business cards as "seer"—next to "accountant," of course. Her interest in the occult was more than just a passing phase. She did palm readings, tarot spreads and the like for extra cash, but the truth was that her abilities were based more on an uncanny knack for reading people's expressions and intuiting what they needed to hear than any real premonitory gift.

Cass had told her frequently that it was better that way. Knowing the future wasn't all it was cracked up to be, especially if the future wasn't so shiny. And in Cass's experience, no one ever seemed to believe what she saw—or *felt*, as the case may be—anyway. Emma's method was much more successful, but she never saw it that way. Her envy of Cass's Sight was good-natured, but it was there all the same.

"Regardless," Emma said, steering the conversation back to the brownie in the entryway, "do you really think a colander will work to keep it out?"

"It should. It's a trick Aunt Alexandra picked up when she visited Greece." Alexandra had been quite the world traveler in her youth, and Greece had always been one of her favorite places. She often said she would have loved to settle down there, but for some reason or other, she felt the need to stay here. Cass couldn't imagine why. A sun-soaked island seemed a much better retirement spot than this decrepit old logging town.

"That's what I'm saying," said Emma. "Your aunt also had the Sight, right? So she obviously knew they were there. She must have kept them around for a reason. If she hadn't wanted them there, wouldn't she have done something to keep them out?"

"Yeah, well, she's not here anymore," Cass snapped. A sharp pang jabbed in her chest as she said it, and hot tears pricked behind her eyes. She blinked them away. There was no point sugar-coating it. Aunt Alexandra was gone, and it wasn't going to do her any good to ignore the fact. "And it's not like she left an instruction booklet. This is my house now, and I'm not going to sleep well at night if there are all sorts of weird little creatures in here."

As if on cue, Onyx strutted into the room and looked at Cass suspiciously. Befitting his name, he was pure black, with long, silky fur. She held out her fingers for him to sniff, but he turned his nose up and flounced under the plush armchair next to the fireplace. That relationship was off to a good start.

"Well, what's the rest of the house like?" asked Emma.

Cass shrugged, though Emma couldn't see her. "Cluttered, from what I could tell. I didn't go through the whole house yet, though. Some of the rooms upstairs were locked, and so was the door to that tower thing. I'm going to have to look around for the keys, or else get the locks changed."

"So you don't even know what's in there? Creepy. For all you know, there could be, like, dead bodies or something."

"Real reassuring, Em." Cass tossed the last book in her stack onto the giveaway pile and stood up shakily, her legs stiff from sitting on the floor for the last half hour. One stack down. Only about a million more to go. "Look, I probably ought to get going. I've got a huge mess to deal with, plus I still need to get groceries and stuff."

"All right. But keep me posted if you *see* anything else, okay?"

Cass rolled her eyes but agreed, and Emma hung up. Cass brushed off the knees of her jeans and looked around the room. It seemed even messier now than it had before she started. She squeezed her eyes closed to keep from feeling overwhelmed.

Aunt Alexandra, why did you leave me with all this? she thought. But she knew the answer. It hadn't been a surprise. She'd told Cass she was planning on leaving her the house for years. "You are the only one I trust with my things, Cassie," she'd often said on the phone, a tone of gentle exasperation in her voice. "Your father doesn't understand. He doesn't know. You know. You're the only one who will know what to do with this house."

No, the bigger surprise had been that Alexandra had passed at all. She'd gone quietly in her sleep at the age of ninety-four, which was a blessing but also a shock. Despite her age, she'd been healthy and strong. She'd seemed eternal. Cass had spent the last several weeks cursing herself that she'd never gotten around to visiting her again. It had been years since the last time she'd seen her, though they talked on the phone every week. When Alexandra was younger, they used to travel together—visiting far-off cities and exotic locations, just the two of them. Seeing the world and its secrets in a way that only they could. But eventually, Alexandra had become content to remain in her big old house in the woods, while Cass wanted to keep wandering.

Or running, maybe.

Cass sighed and left the book room behind, heading into the kitchen to assess the food situation. It looked like someone— probably Connie—had come through already and removed all the perishables. All that was left was some dried pasta and a few cans that looked as though they'd been sitting in Alexandra's pantry for about as long as she'd lived there.

Onyx trailing a safe distance behind her, Cass grabbed her purse and car keys and started out the kitchen door. She hesitated for a moment as the cat watched her with bright green eyes. "Are you an outdoor kitty or an indoor kitty?" she asked.

Onyx made a noise that sounded like "*Myah.*"

Cass smirked. "Sorry, didn't catch that. I think I'd better leave you inside just in case." She closed and locked the door.

She could feel eyes following her as she wound her way along the side of the house back to the front drive where her car was parked. The yard was dotted with clumps of trees that had been there so long they'd started to grow into each other, and out of the corner of her eye, she could see faces among the needles, peering around the leaves. Green, bronze, brown and gold; squat and round, with bulbous noses; long and narrow with pointed ears that protruded through mossy tufts of hair. There had to be a dozen different species of fae in there. The air was heavy with their magic, and it made her skin crawl.

"It's an infestation," she grumbled, avoiding looking at the creatures directly.

The front lawn was littered with dry needles and pieces of pinecone that crunched under her shoes. She kept her gaze on her feet, stubbornly ignoring the prying eyes in the trees. As she walked, she noticed a glint of color among the greens and browns. She paused, wrinkling her nose, and crouched to examine it more closely. A card, covered in a blue plaid pattern. It was longer than a regular playing card. She picked it up and flipped it over. A tarot card. It looked like one of Emma's. Cass didn't know much about tarot. Like everything else supernatural, she tried to avoid it as much as she could. This card had a picture of a man in vaguely medieval-looking clothing, like a minstrel, or maybe a jester. He was holding a white flower in his left hand, and in his right was a long stick with a pack or something attached to it. It reminded Cass of old cartoons, when characters would run away from home carrying a knapsack on a stick. A small white dog yapped at the man's feet. The two of them looked very happy—even though they were about to blunder right off the edge of a cliff. The text underneath the picture read: *The Fool.*

"Well, that's interesting," she said aloud. She straightened, then froze. She *felt* something. Someone was watching her. Not the fae—a person. Human. She looked around warily. There was a rustle, and then the sound of a branch snapping. She turned just in time to catch a glimpse of black hair disappearing behind a tree trunk, and the swish of a skirt. A girl?

"Excuse me?" Cass called. No one responded. She sighed and took a few steps closer to the patch of trees. "Hey, sorry, this is private property," she said.

Still no answer. Then the leaves rustled again, and a little green creature shimmied its way down the tree trunk, planting its feet firmly on a gnarled root. Cass had never seen a creature quite like this one before. She didn't recognize its species. It was bigger than the other fae she'd seen, with a long, pointed nose and pronounced cheekbones. The top of its head was covered with leaves, which could have been a hat or the creature's own hair.

It folded its arms and looked at Cass appraisingly, unflinchingly. Its stare seemed to be a challenge—one that Cass didn't feel like rising to.

"Okay, whatever," she said, turning back to her car and unlocking the door. "Have it your way."

She tossed the tarot card onto the passenger seat next to her purse. Something about it made her feel uneasy, but for some reason, she was reluctant to throw it away. It didn't look like it had been outside long—it was pretty clean, and relatively new-looking. Probably not one of Aunt Alexandra's; Cass knew she had a few decks, but they were all much older than this. Had that strange girl dropped it?

She looked around for the intruder as she pulled her car down the driveway, but there was no sign of her. She must have retreated deeper into Alexandra's property According to the surveyor's records her aunt's lawyer had shown her, Alexandra's property encompassed almost a hundred acres of winding forest land. A few houses dotted the perimeter—maybe it had been one of the neighbors. Although it was strange that she'd run away instead of introducing herself...

"This whole freaking place is weird," Cass said aloud, turning from her driveway onto the narrow logging road that led into town. To her left, she could see Connie's ranch-style home peeking out between the trees. A mailbox adorned with cheery painted flowers sat next to the driveway.

She struggled to remember if the presence of the fae had been this strong when she'd last visited this house. She'd probably only been ten or eleven at that time. Twenty years had dulled her memory, and she found that when she thought about it, she could only remember snatches—the purple paint on the big Victorian house had stood out in her mind, and the smell of the kitchen. Alexandra showing her photos from her last visit to Budapest. But most of the details had faded away with time.

It wasn't unusual for fae to turn up in large quantities in wooded areas, she reminded herself. She just wasn't used to it anymore, having spent so much time in large cities. Like it did with most wildlife, modernity did a good job of crowding the supernatural out.

"The sooner I can get out of here and back to the city, the better," Cass grumbled, flipping on her blinker and turning onto Main Street.

Something that she *did* remember from her last visit, and which still seemed to be true, was that there wasn't a real supermarket in Riddle—just a tiny general store next to the post office. But she didn't feel like driving to Myrtle Creek, where the closest Safeway was located, so Riddle Grocery would have to do.

It hadn't changed much in twenty years. Cass suspected that it hadn't changed much in forty years, to be honest. It was a small wood-frame building with weathered gray siding. There was a huge Pepsi logo next to the sign over the door, and a hand-painted board in the window reading, "*Proudly serving Pepsi products!*"

"Guess I'd better not think about buying a Coca-Cola," Cass said to herself, pulling the white wooden door open.

Inside, it looked just like a regular grocery store, albeit on a smaller scale. As soon as she stepped through the door, she realized she'd made a tactical error, coming to the grocery store on an empty stomach. The smell of warm food wafted toward her from the deli, and suddenly she found she could think of nothing else but fried chicken and potato wedges.

"Priorities, Cass," she told herself, grabbing a small shopping cart with a squeaking wheel from beside the front door. "Get your groceries first. *Then* you can hit the deli."

She pushed past the front lanes, such as they were—just a couple counters with cash registers and a lone cashier who smiled and nodded as she went by—and headed for the refrigerated section. She'd need milk, butter, eggs... and it couldn't hurt to buy some TV dinners. Okay, several TV dinners. Or, as she preferred to think of them, Meals For One. As she turned into the frozen foods aisle, her eye caught on something sitting atop one of the freezers. A large plush dog, white with floppy brown ears and a splotch of brown over one of its plastic eyes. There was a piece of paper around its neck, laminated and printed with the words, "*Congratulations! You found the White-and-Brown Dog! Now go to the library and tell the librarian where you found me.*"

Cass raised an eyebrow. One of her soon-to-be colleagues at the Riddle Library must be responsible for this—they must have been running some kind of summer scavenger hunt program for the local kids. She felt her stomach twist slightly with nerves. She'd worked at various libraries over the years, but generally large systems in bigger cities. Her last job had been at the San Jose Public Library. She'd been ready for a change when she'd gotten the news about Aunt Alexandra—though she tended to thrive in urban environments, the California Bay Area was a bit much even for her—but she still wasn't sure this change was really what she had in mind. She'd thought it was a long shot when she contacted the Douglas County library system to see if they needed a short-term librarian, and had been shocked when they informed her that there was an open slot right there at the Riddle branch library. It had seemed too good to be true, and now Cass found herself wondering if maybe it was. This was a small town, and she was sure the other librarians must have lived in the community their whole lives. How would they react to having a stranger like Cass coming in out of nowhere?

She tossed a handful of Lean Cuisines into her cart and turned away from the White-and-Brown Dog and into the next aisle. This was another mistake—the junk food aisle. The shelves were lined with chips, cookies, and other packaged sweets of the partially-hydrogenated variety. Her stomach rumbled as her eye fell on a box of chocolate MoonPies on the top shelf. She hadn't had them for years. They weren't even her favorite snack, with their somewhat rubbery consistency, but right now they seemed like the perfect complement to that fried chicken and those potato wedges that she'd determined were going to be her late-lunch/early-dinner.

She stretched her hand up to grab for the box, but her fingertips just grazed it. Cass was of average height—usually tall enough to be able to reach the top shelf, but that typically relied on her wearing a set of shoes with thicker soles than these beat-up, flattened flip-flops she was wearing today. She frowned, looking around. Riddle Grocery didn't seem to be particularly overstaffed. She supposed she could ask the cashier if he could come grab them for her, but by the same token, hadn't she had enough human interaction for today?

She got up on her tiptoes, stretching once more for the MoonPies. Her fingers brushed the box again... just enough to make the box tip back and topple. Before she could react, the MoonPies had created a domino effect, knocking the boxes that were behind it over. She could just see the top of a box of cereal on the top shelf of the next aisle over wobble, and then it fell with a crash, bringing several other boxes down with it. A cry of surprise rang out from the next aisle.

Great. *Just* great. Someone had been here to catch her moment of epic poise.

She left her cart behind, hurrying over to the cereal aisle, calling out, "I'm so sorry"—but she broke off at the sight of the man standing in the middle of the aisle surrounded by a pile of fallen Cheerios, Frosted Flakes and Wheaties boxes. He looked to be about Cass's age, thirty or so. Tall and muscular, but lean rather than broad, with honey-brown hair and eyes to match. Clean-shaven—a rarity among millennial men, Cass had found, and particularly in Oregon—wearing a fitted plaid button-down shirt, the sleeves rolled halfway up his forearm, revealing lightly tanned skin and large, square hands.

It had been a long time since the sight of a man had made Cass lose her voice, but this one had definitely succeeded. She cleared her throat, hoping her face wasn't too visibly red, and said again, "I'm so sorry."

The man laughed, gentle creases forming around his warm eyes, and Cass found she needed to clear her throat again. "No worries," he said. "That was an impressive avalanche. Do you need help with something?"

"No, no," Cass said quickly. "It's fine. Let me get these picked up." She crouched, hurrying to gather all the cereal boxes up into her arms, taking more than she really could hold at once, causing her to drop a few with another loud crash. The man laughed again, moving to help her. Between the two of them, the cereal shelf was quickly righted, save one box of Cheerios Cass grabbed for herself.

"There. No harm done," the man said with a grin, his bright white teeth practically sparkling in the fluorescent lighting overhead. Cass could only dream of such white teeth herself. She drank too much coffee and tea without brushing afterward, and never seemed to have any luck with over-the-counter whitening kits and toothpastes. "You're sure you don't need help getting anything?"

"I'm fine, thanks," Cass said, offering him a tight smile. The man nodded and she returned to her shopping cart, her heart racing. She tried to focus on getting the rest of her groceries, but she found she couldn't concentrate—the store was too small, and she kept passing the honey-haired man in every aisle, her pulse quickening every time they passed each other. It really was ridiculous, the way he was making her react. What was she, fourteen? She'd seen handsome men before. Granted, it had been a long time since she'd seen one *this* handsome. But honestly.

After she passed the refrigerator of eggs three times without seeing them, she decided to give up. She had her milk and a box of Cheerios, that was good enough to get her through breakfast tomorrow. She'd come back to get the rest another time. Or maybe she *would* make the drive to Myrtle Creek and go to Safeway instead.

Brushing past the man yet again—trying her best not to look at him—she made her way to the far wall of the small store, where the deli was located. "What can I get you?" asked a friendly older man wearing a paper overseas cap and an apron.

"Could I get two fried chicken legs and a half-pound of potato wedges, please?" Cass said. She watched as the man wrapped the chicken in brown paper and scooped the potato wedges into a cardboard container, weighing them on a metal food scale. In the reflected glass of the deli counter, she saw movement behind her, and she turned to see the man from the cereal aisle push past. She thought for a dreaded moment that he was going to order from the deli, too, and her face grew hot at the thought of being in his proximity yet *again*. But he just smiled and moved away, disappearing back between the shelves.

It wasn't until she made it to the cashier and started unloading her groceries and the two deli items onto the counter that she realized there was something extra in her cart: a box of chocolate MoonPies.

Cass looked around the store, but the man with the honey-brown hair was nowhere to be seen.

Chapter 3

The honey-haired man didn't leave Cass's mind for the rest of the afternoon. He was firmly rooted in her subconscious as she sorted more books, taking care to keep a handkerchief between her fingers—still greasy from the chicken and potato wedges—and the books' dusty spines. And he stayed there even after she gave up on book sorting for the day and went into the kitchen, where Onyx danced around her feet in anticipation of his dinner. Still full from her fried-food feast, she dished up a saucer of wet food for Onyx—who knew exactly where it should go, guiding her, screaming the whole way, over to a little mat in front of the cupboards beside the kitchen sink—and then sat at the table in the breakfast nook, gazing out at the darkening yard, trying *not* to think of the man from the grocery store... and failing miserably.

The box of MoonPies sat unopened on the kitchen counter behind her. It had been very thoughtful of him to grab them for her even though she'd told him not to bother. But his thoughtfulness just made it all the worse. Cass had promised herself long ago that she wasn't going to let another man get under her skin. Not after what had happened the last time. And it had worked. For five years, it had worked. So why was this one guy affecting her so much?

Stop, she told herself. It didn't matter how handsome *or* thoughtful he was. It wouldn't work out. It never worked out for Cass, and with good reason. Besides, he was probably married. She hadn't gotten a look at his left hand to see if there was a ring there—not that that necessarily would have mattered, anyway, considering that not everyone wore a ring—but Connie had said most people tended to marry young in the Pacific Northwest, and it was something Cass herself had noticed during her brief period living in Seattle. The odds of there being a hot, considerate, *single* man her age in Riddle, Oregon, population one thousand, were close to zero.

So she needed to stop thinking about him.

Finally, after Onyx had finished his dinner and begun bathing his whiskers, and what she could see of the sky between the trees had faded from blazing red to dusky purple, Cass wandered upstairs, trying to decide which room she should sleep in that night. It seemed wrong to take Aunt Alexandra's room—the room where her great-aunt had spent every night, the bed where she'd *died* (Cass tried not to let her mind dwell on that)—so she opted for the guest room she remembered sleeping in as a child.

It was a large room, especially for a secondary bedroom. She vaguely remembered Aunt Alexandra telling her about the original owners of this house, and that they'd been quite wealthy—wealthy enough to afford such a big house, with big rooms for everyone in the household, even the servants whose quarters were in the finished attic. This room had walls papered in a light spring green with small white flowers embossed in the silk. The brass bed was neatly made with an eyelet coverlet across the top. Though she knew this room had been unoccupied, there was no dust anywhere, and the bedding smelled fresh, not musty. Faded white wainscoting covered the lower half of the walls, and a white marble fireplace took up part of one wall. Cass was sure that would be wonderful in the winter, but tonight just the thought of it made her feel ill. Despite its reputation among out-of-staters for being a rainy state, most of Oregon got quite hot in the summer, and Riddle was no exception. Now, in late August, the house, with no air conditioning, was sweltering.

Cass opened the three windows on the east wall, revealing the sliver of the rising moon peeking between the trees; then she opened the transom over her bedroom door to let air flow in from the cool, dark hallway—or so she hoped, anyway. The room still felt oppressively warm, though. She went back downstairs to where she'd left her suitcase in the entryway, then dragged it up and into the second-floor bathroom. Though the bathroom itself was original to the house, the fixtures had been replaced in the forties, and it showed. The bathtub and the sink were *pink*, and the linoleum floor was in dire need of replacement. Cass hoped that might be something she could fob off on the buyers, since she certainly couldn't afford a bathroom renovation on her librarian salary. She changed into her pajamas, a spaghetti-strap tank top and a pair of plaid boy shorts, and she pulled her dark hair back into a ponytail. That helped cool her off a little. She splashed some water on her face and then went back to her bedroom.

Onyx was in there now, sitting on top of the radiator, his attention fixed on the window. He sat stock-still, no part of his body moving except for the absolute tip of his tail, which twitched and flicked in agitation. At the sight of him, her skin began to crawl. "Oh, great, now what?" she said aloud.

She went over to the window to see what he was staring at, fully expecting to find some disgusting magical creature—another brownie, or maybe an elf—prowling along the sill. Her muscles tense, she came up behind the cat and followed his gaze, then breathed out a sigh of relief when she saw it wasn't anything supernatural. It was a beetle, small and brown and speckled. A stink bug. The house would probably be overrun with them come fall; they always wanted to come inside for the winter. Slightly less irritating than the fae, but only just.

"Leave it alone," she chided the cat, scooping the beetle up. "The last thing you want is a face full of stink spray." She tossed the bug out the open window and then froze. Eyes were watching her between the leaves of a nearby tree. She stared back at them, and after a moment she recognized the face from earlier. It was the little green fae, the one who'd been there when she was leaving for the grocery store. She'd never seen anything like this creature before. Longer, pointier features than a brownie or gnome, but lacking the telltale wings of a faery or pixy. And that coloring! She wondered what species it was.

"You're not coming in here," she said to the creature. It raised its eyebrows as if to say, *Oh, really? And what's going to stop me?*

She frowned at the unspoken question. After all, there were no screens on these windows—there really wasn't anything to stop it coming in. She sighed wearily and closed all three of the open windows.

That just made the room grow even hotter, though. Cass lay on the bed, not bothering to pull the covers back; it was going to be way too warm for that tonight. Even though she had no plans on staying here longer than it took to sort out Aunt Alexandra's belongings and sell the house, she found herself making a mental list of improvements. First, screens on all the windows, to keep out all the pests—of both the normal and magical variety. Second, replace the pendant lamp in this room with a ceiling fan. She knew installing air conditioning in a house of this size would be out of the question, especially on her budget, but days like this made it tempting. Maybe a swamp cooler would suffice.

She lay there, uncomfortable, her shirt drenched in sweat and her mind a tumult of thoughts—thoughts of Aunt Alexandra, of the house, of everything she still had left to do; of starting work at the library; of the fae just outside her window; of the guy from the grocery store. She couldn't get her mind to settle down enough to be willing to pick up a book, or even browse her phone. An hour passed, and she felt nowhere near sleepy. She just felt ungodly hot.

"Forget it," she said, sitting up. "I'll just go back downstairs and sort more stupid books. It's not like I don't get enough of that at work—" She broke off mid-rant at the sight of a flash of color on the mantel of the white marble fireplace.

That wasn't there before.

It was a tarot card, like the one she'd found outside. She'd forgotten all about it after everything that had happened at the grocery store. It was still lying, she assumed, in the passenger seat of her car. But as she drew closer, she saw that this couldn't be the same card, anyway—it had a different image on it. This one depicted a woman in a long dress, sitting in a large chair—or maybe a throne? She had a crown of flowers and stars on her head, and held a scepter in her right hand. The text at the bottom of the card read: *The Empress.*

Cass felt her skin crawl once again. This was getting ridiculous. She couldn't remember this ever happening before, so many premonitions in one day. Usually they were spaced out enough that she'd have time to process them, to intuit what they were trying to tell her, but it had been almost incessant ever since she got into Riddle: the feeling that *something* was going to happen, but she didn't know what. And considering that her bad feelings usually translated to bad *things* happening to *someone*, not being able to figure out what these feelings were trying to tell her made her especially nervous.

She ran a sticky hand through her hair. She needed to get out of this oven of a bedroom. Without thinking about it any further, she shoved her feet into the same flip-flops she'd worn earlier and walked briskly down the stairs. But she didn't return to the room she'd been sorting books in, the parlor-turned-Library-Number-One. Instead, she opened the front door and stalked out into the night.

The air outside was at least ten degrees cooler than it had been inside her room, and the relief was instantaneous. The moon was higher now, but the summer sky was not quite dark. It was a little before ten o'clock; still early enough to justify a before-bed walk to clear her head.

She circled the perimeter of the overgrown yard. A number of trails forked away from the house and into the woods, edged with uneven, moss-covered stones that kept the mess of ferns and groundcover from spilling onto the dirt paths. Cass chose one at random, clutching her phone tightly in case the trail got too dark or—in a worst-case scenario—she needed to call for help.

The trail led her down a gently-sloping hill and into a clearing that she assumed must have once been a garden. In its center was a crumbling stone fountain. Giant, unkempt rose bushes had grown up higher than Cass's head, their woody canes covered in wickedly sharp thorns. In the moonlight, the reds and oranges of their flowers were muted. Cass noticed that many of the bushes had more hips than blooms now. Fall was approaching, even if today's weather seemed to indicate otherwise.

A set of overgrown stone steps led out of the garden, and Cass followed them into the ever-deepening woods. The trees were tall, the black silhouettes of their trunks rising into the night sky. Giant oak trees with gnarled branches intertwined above her head, forming a canopy that during the day would likely look charming, but tonight left Cass feeling unsettled. These trees were wild. She'd never felt anything like this before. The air was thick, heavy with magic, making goosebumps ripple across her skin and a lump form in the pit of her stomach. Some distant part of her mind wondered if she should turn back, but her feet kept on going, dreamlike.

There was a light ahead. At first she thought it was the light of the moon drifting through the entangled branches, but after a time Cass realized that the moon had been behind her earlier. Had the trail wound around in a circle, or was it something else? As she walked, she became distantly aware of the sounds around her, different than the regular sounds of the forest. Was that the hoot of an owl, or a hoot of laughter? Nightingale song, or human voices singing? The rustling of leaves, or... feet... dancing? The light before her seemed to change, moving, shifting colors. The circle of the moon widened, separated. Became a ring. A ring of dancing, glowing lights. Music, laughter, inviting her in. She stepped forward as if in a haze.

A branch swung down, smacking her hard across her face.

"Ow!" Cass cried out, looking around herself. The ring of light had vanished. Now only the moon remained.

"What in the world?" she breathed aloud.

"You need to watch yourself. You were being pixy-led."

The voice was high, reedy. She couldn't tell if it was male or female. She jumped, looking around, trying to find the source of the voice.

There, sitting in the fork of an oak to her left, was the green fae. She wouldn't have seen it at all were it not for the soft glow around its tiny body.

Cass blinked, staring at it. Had that creature just spoken to her in English? It was impossible.

The creature snickered. "If that's what you want to believe," it said.

Her eyes widened, and she took a step closer. "How...?" She'd never heard any of the magical creatures she'd encountered before speaking anything but that strange woodland language she could never understand. How had this one learned English?

The fae didn't answer. It just smiled, quirking its head at her, staring at her in an extremely discomfiting way—as if it could see her from the inside out.

She shook her head, looking away. "I wasn't being pixy-led," she asserted.

"You were."

She stubbornly crossed her arms. "I've been dealing with you pests for thirty years. I know better than to be pixy-led."

"If that's what you want to believe."

Cass stamped her foot in frustration. She wasn't going to give in to this... *thing.* Whatever it was. And she certainly wasn't going to acknowledge that she knew it was probably right—the faery ring she'd seen, the way she'd been moving as if she were in a trance, those were all definite signs of being led astray by fae of some sort. How had she walked so neatly into their trap? Why did the magic of the fae seem to be so much stronger here than anywhere else she'd been?

"Because these woods are different," the green creature said. She looked at it sharply, and it smirked. "You know it's true. You've felt it. There's no hiding from it. It's inside you. You recognize the way this place makes you feel."

"Whatever," Cass said, turning on her heel and striding back in the direction she'd come in. The fae didn't follow her, and the numbing sensation of the magic she'd felt on the trail soon vanished. Once she had her bearings back, she realized she'd walked much, much farther than she'd thought. The return trip seemed to take ages, and when she was back at the house, her calves ached and her feet were weeping from the strain she'd put them through, walking so far on uneven terrain in flip-flops. She paused on the stoop and pressed the lock button on her phone. The screen lit up to show her the time—well past midnight. The pixies had led her astray for over two hours. She cursed, kicking the colander on the porch aside before flinging the front door open. Onyx was sitting on the bottom step of the staircase, watching her as she stormed into the house.

"If that green thing comes in here tonight," she told the cat, "I expect you to eat it. Understand?" Onyx's only response was a blink, which Cass hoped was the cat's way of agreeing.

She slammed the door behind her, pushing against it with her hip. With a scrape and a squeal, the deadbolt turned, locking her inside.

But somehow she got the feeling it wouldn't be locking anything *out*.

Chapter 4

The next morning, the doorbell rang early.

Cass was awake, at least, sitting at the kitchen table staring off into space—and wondering if there was any coffee to be found in this house—while Onyx gobbled down his breakfast. He'd been the one who woke her this morning, poking her cheek with one claw over and over until she finally snapped into consciousness. He'd had a list of demands for her. The first was that she scoop his litterbox, which she found in a corner of the downstairs bathroom with a plastic scoop stored neatly beside it. He'd guided her there, making persistent little grunting sounds in the back of his throat until he was satisfied that it was pristine. Once he'd ensured that the litter inside was nice and clean—hopping into the box and poking and prodding around to make absolutely certain—he christened it, and then led her into the kitchen to demand his breakfast. It was clear who ruled the roost around here.

When the doorbell rang, Cass's first inclination was to ignore it. But when it rang a second time, she decided to creep to the front of the house as quietly as she could to see who it was without having to commit herself to answering.

No such luck, though. When she reached the entryway, she saw a man's face peeking through the beveled glass window beside the door. She wasn't sure he'd seen her, but then he said loudly, "Good morning, Ms. Russo! I hope I didn't wake you."

Creeper much? she thought in irritation before opening the door. The man was older, probably around her parents' age, and wearing a suit. "No, you didn't," she said. "How can I help you?"

"The name's Kowalski. Tom Kowalski. I own the property that borders yours to the north."

"Oh. Nice to meet you, Mr. Kowalski," Cass said after a moment, relaxing. From the way he was dressed, she'd been worried he was someone from her aunt's law firm, that there was some sort of problem. This was just a neighbor, probably trying to be friendly. Though what kind of neighbor would think it was appropriate to be friendly before nine o'clock on a Sunday, she didn't know.

"Yes, yes," he said, adjusting his tie, and Cass got the distinct impression he was thinking, *Of course it's nice to meet me. I'm aware of my own excellence.* She wondered if all of Aunt Alexandra's neighbors were as odd as Connie and this Kowalski person. "Anyway, I won't waste your time—let me get straight to the point. My understanding is that you're not intending to make Riddle your permanent home?"

Good *grief*, did these people have anything better to do with their time than gossip? "No, I'm not," she said with a tight smile. "I'm here for a few months to sort out my aunt's things, but I won't be staying beyond that."

"Excellent," Mr. Kowalski said, surprising her. That was the exact opposite of the reaction she'd gotten from Connie. "Ms. Russo, I'd like to make an offer on this property. How does one million dollars sound?"

Cass choked. She wasn't sure what she even choked on—the air? Her saliva? The words coming out of Mr. Kowalski's mouth? She didn't know, but suddenly she was coughing her lungs out, shaking her head as Mr. Kowalski stepped forward to offer help. She braced herself on the doorjamb. Had she heard him correctly? A *million* dollars? Was he insane? She knew it was a lot of land, but the lawyer had indicated to her that with the condition of the house and grounds, she shouldn't expect more than $400,000 or so. Kowalski was offering her well over twice that amount. What was the catch? There had to be a catch. Even though a big part of her was screaming *Take the money!* an even larger part was urging caution—and suspicion.

"I'm sorry," she said once she'd regained her breath. "I haven't really thought about selling yet. Everything has been happening so fast..." She shrugged in what she hoped was a conciliatory way.

Mr. Kowalski smiled, though it didn't quite reach his eyes. "Of course. I understand. There's no rush. You can get in touch with me once you've had a chance to think it over." He pulled a leather wallet out of his back trouser pocket and withdrew a business card from it, handing it to her. Cass glanced down to see a logo of a stylized mountain top. It read *Cow Creek Investments* in a bold sans-serif typeface, and below that, *Tom Kowalski, CEO.*

"If you get any alternative offers, please let me know," he said. "I would be happy to negotiate. This property means a lot to me. I know it did to your aunt as well. I'd hate to see it fall into the hands of someone who doesn't... *appreciate* it as much as it deserves."

Cass furrowed her brows as Mr. Kowalski turned and started back down the steps. It was only as he moved away from her that she saw he wasn't alone—a second figure hovered at the bottom of the steps. A little girl, probably around eight or nine years old. She was crouched, looking into the overgrown flowerbed next to the stoop.

"Lily, come on," Mr. Kowalski snapped, and she jumped up, her shoulder-length black hair whipping around her face as she moved. As it did, a wave of recognition washed over Cass. Black hair through the branches of the trees. Was this girl the one who'd been watching her yesterday?

Before turning to follow Mr. Kowalski, she glanced up at Cass. In her hands was the metal colander that Cass had kicked into the bushes last night. She smiled shyly, setting it down on the steps before hurrying after Mr. Kowalski—her father, Cass assumed.

Cass watched them climb into a sleek black sedan. Once it had pulled out of her driveway and disappeared down the road, she gingerly made her way—barefoot—down the pine needle-covered steps and picked up the colander. Goosebumps ran across her skin. Were they because of Mr. Kowalski, or the girl? Or was it just this weird reaction she'd been having ever since she arrived in Riddle?

She looked around to see if that odd green fae was anywhere around. But she saw nothing. She sighed and carried the colander back into the house.

"That's it, I'm coming to Riddle," Em said firmly over the phone.

Cass rolled her eyes. Her friend's eagerness had nothing to do with Tom Kowalski and his million-dollar offer—she'd barely paid any attention to that. It was Cass's account of the events of the night before that held all the appeal to Emma.

"You can't just drop everything and come here," Cass said.

"I can and I will!"

"Emma," Cass said, laughing, "you just used up all your vacation time visiting me in California. What are you going to tell your boss, 'Sorry, I need a second vacation two months after my last one because I need to go investigate the paranormal activity in Middle-of-Nowhere, Oregon'?"

"I could tell him 'I quit.'"

Cass looked at her phone in alarm. "Emma, you can't quit your job over this!"

Emma sighed in a long-suffering way. "I guess you're right. But this is so unfair. You've had more supernatural sightings in the last twenty-four hours than you usually have in a year!"

"Ugh, I know. This is why I stay in urban environments. Fae need trees to thrive. Old, established trees. Those are few and far between in the concrete jungle. I should never have agreed to this," Cass moaned.

Em made a tutting sound, and Cass knew she was once again wishing they could trade places. *Believe me*, she thought, *if I could, I would in an instant.*

Finally, changing the subject, Emma said, "I want to know about those tarot cards you found. That's different. Do you think the fae could have left them for you?"

"I guess? But you're right, it's not their typical M.O.," Cass said. "They're usually known for *taking* things, not leaving them. Well, maybe household elves... but still, this doesn't seem like a household elf thing, either. The whole thing just feels weird." Like that green creature in the woods last night.

"The first card you found in the yard—describe it for me," Em commanded.

"*The Fool*. Some medieval-y guy walking off a cliff with his dog."

"That's the first card in the major arcana. It usually signifies the beginning of a journey," Emma explained.

"Well, that could be a good sign," Cass said. "Maybe it means as soon as I offload this house, I'm going on an adventure." If she took Tom Kowalski up on his offer, she could afford to take a nice trip—maybe visit Greece in Aunt Alexandra's memory. She frowned, not sure how she felt about that idea.

"Maybe. It can be hard to tell when the cards appear individually rather than in a spread. What about the other one?" Cass described the imagery on the card she'd found on the fireplace, *The Empress*. "Hmm," said Emma. "I don't know about that."

Cass felt the skin on her arms begin to prickle. "Why? What does that mean?"

"It's the motherhood card. It usually represents a mother figure, or maybe a pregnancy."

Cass choked on nothing again. "Excuse me?" she spluttered between violent coughs. "I don't think so!" But what if it meant something was going to happen to her own mom? Should she take it literally? She'd have to call her mother later. Not that she could warn her—just like practically everyone else she'd met, her mom had never believed Cass about any of her premonitions, so she'd learned to stop telling her about them a while ago. But maybe she could poke around sort of nonchalantly, find out if she and her dad were planning any trips or if she'd been to the doctor recently...

"Well, it does have another meaning, though it's kind of more obscure," Emma went on. "Sometimes it represents nature, a need to get outside to clear one's head."

Cass sighed loudly in relief. "That must be it," she said eagerly. "The card appeared right before I went for my walk last night."

Emma let out another *hmm*, but Cass refused to allow her to elaborate.

"Well, thanks for your help, Em. I'll keep you posted," she quickly said before Emma got a chance to say anything else. "Talk to you later, okay? Bye!" She tapped the *end call* button even as Emma began to protest on the other end of the line. Then she shoved her phone in her pocket and exhaled. This was insane. Weird neighbors, fae everywhere, bizarrely prescient tarot cards materializing out of thin air? Life in Riddle was turning out to be way more complicated than Cass had bargained for.

She couldn't *wait* to see what would be in store for her on her first day of work tomorrow.

Chapter 5

The next day, Cass stood outside the locked doors of the Riddle Library sipping muddy-tasting coffee from a travel mug and wincing after every swallow. She'd been so flustered at the grocery store the other day she'd forgotten to get coffee for herself, or even flavored creamer to add to the ancient off-brand grounds she'd found in the back of Aunt Alexandra's pantry. No amount of sugar would be able to counteract this taste, but she needed the caffeine to function this morning, so she kept doggedly sipping.

She'd slept terribly. Pre-first-day-of-work jitters were normal and she usually had trouble sleeping whenever she had to go somewhere new the next day, but last night had been worse than usual. The sleep she had gotten was restless and fitful, racked with strange dreams about faery rings and a tiny green creature that watched her every move. Most of the dreams had faded as she'd jerked awake, looking at her clock to find that only five minutes had passed since the last nightmare she'd woken from. But one dream stayed with her, and it hung over her like a dark cloud even now in the sun-bright morning. It had featured the honey-haired man from the grocery store.

Prominently featured him.

She didn't even know his name, but that hadn't mattered in the dream. Her face grew hot at the memory of his dream-self lying beside her atop the eyelet bedspread in the Victorian's guest room, her face resting against his chest, dozing while he read a book late into the night. His ghostly lips brushing lightly against hers, stirring her awake. The warmth and familiarity of it, like he'd been there before, like they'd done this thousands of times. Like he belonged there. And then the dream had shifted, to them walking through the overgrown woods, fingers entwined. After a moment Cass had realized they weren't alone. A little girl, eight or nine years old, skipped along beside them. Cass felt a tug of affection as she looked at the girl, a warmth in her heart that she'd never quite felt before. Though she'd never seen her before, she knew, instinctively, that the girl was hers—theirs.

Love.

Then the girl had turned and smiled at her, and suddenly Cass realized that she did know her. This girl wasn't *hers*, she realized with the odd detachment of a dream. It was Tom Kowalski's daughter. Shoulder-length black hair, cut bluntly with straight bangs to match. Dark, round eyes set into a round face. A plaid skirt and a purple sweater.

They were alone in the woods. The man beside Cass had disappeared. The warmth of his presence faded, leaving cold emptiness in its wake.

"You have to stop him," the girl said, looking down at her feet.

"Stop who?" Cass asked. She noticed they'd stopped in front of a massive oak tree, gnarled and sprawling with limbs that forked in every direction. The ground at her feet was lumpy and uneven from the tree's deep roots. Here and there they poked up from the ground, wooden loops like foot snares.

"The warren must not be disturbed. Our retribution will be swift."

Cass started, searching for the origin of the voice. Finding nothing, she looked back at the girl, only to see the small green creature perched on her shoulder like a pet bird.

"What's the warren?" Cass asked.

The girl didn't seem to notice the creature on her shoulder. She looked up at Cass now. Her eyes had darkened, the pupils round as saucers and black as midnight. "If you don't stop him, we'll all die."

Cass couldn't look away from her eyes. The darkness in them was growing. Any second it would swallow them all up.

"Who—?"

"*We'll all die.*"

Cass had woken with a start, drenched in sweat, her legs tangled in the sheets. Her skin was covered in goosebumps, and the usual premonitory lump in her stomach felt more like a developing ulcer. A muted gray light was streaming in through the sheer curtains.

"That's it," she'd said, sitting bolt upright. Onyx had been curled tightly in the farthest corner of the bed, and at her sudden movement he'd rocketed away, splayed claws *scritch*-ing noisily across the hardwood floor. She flung the covers aside. No more attempting to sleep. Good morning, five A.M.

She'd gotten up, taken a long shower to clear her head, and begun searching the kitchen high and low for coffee—any coffee at all. When she'd finally found the ancient tin of grounds and the even-ancienter coffee pot, she'd brewed herself a travel mug and, after shoveling some cereal into her mouth, headed straight over to the library. No sense prolonging the inevitable.

She took another sip now, sighing. She'd gotten here too early. The library opened at eight o'clock. She figured one of the other librarians would be there by seven-thirty, but she'd figured wrong. There was no one here but Cass and her unwelcome thoughts.

"It usually represents a mother figure, or maybe a pregnancy."

She chewed the inside of her cheek, remembering Emma's words about *The Empress* tarot card. That must have been what had inspired the dream. But Cass was mortified that she'd had such an intense, vivid dream about two complete strangers, no matter how attractive one of them was. And the end of the dream—that really bothered her. That had all the signs of being a genuine premonition. The goosebumps, the lump in the pit of her stomach; she'd been so nauseous when she awoke that for a panicked moment she'd thought she was going to throw up. Classic premonitory symptoms.

But *we'll all die*... that was just a *tad* direr than her usual visions. The only other one she'd ever had that was even remotely on that scale had been—

"I'm sorry, I'm sorry!"

Cass jumped in surprise, sloshing muddy coffee over the sides of the travel mug. She frowned, debating whether to bother rifling through her purse for a Kleenex or just wipe her sticky fingers on the side of her pants, as a tall, slender young woman hurried up to the library door beside her. "Cass, right?" the woman asked. To Cass's relief, she didn't try to shake her coffee-covered hand—she was too busy trying to juggle her own coffee and a set of keys.

"Yeah, I'm Cass. Are you one of the other librarians?"

"Yes, I'm Darcy. Nice to meet you." The woman shoved the keys into the glass door and then turned and gave Cass a little wave. "I'll just be a second. Have to be quick to turn the alarm off or the whole neighborhood will know. Last thing we need is the cops showing up on your first day, right? Not that they have all that far to go," she added, gesturing to the police station across the parking lot from the library.

Darcy shoved the door open with her hip and hurried over to a box on the wall that was beeping loudly. She pressed a few buttons and the beeping stopped. "There,' Darcy said with a sigh and a grin. "Now that that's taken care of. I hope you weren't standing there too long! I was running late. Had to get my fix." She held up a white cardboard coffee cup with a black lid and a sleeve that said *Alice's Pony Espresso* on it.

"Where did you get that?" Cass asked, her eyes widening.

"There's a drive-through coffee place in Myrtle Creek. It's like twenty minutes out of the way, but I'm willing to make the sacrifice. If it means I have to go eighty on the frontage road getting back out here before the library opens, that's a risk I'll have to take."

"I'll probably be right there with you tomorrow," Cass said with a laugh.

Darcy grinned cheerfully, revealing a small gap between her two front teeth. She was probably around Cass's age, but the combination of that smile and the dusting of freckles across her tanned cheeks made her look younger. "Okay, we've technically got five minutes until the library opens, but I doubt it's going to be exactly hopping. We usually get busier in the afternoon, so I can spend most of this morning showing you the ropes."

"Are you the head librarian?" Cass asked.

"Oh, no, that's Randy. He's off today. We usually don't have more than two people working at a time. Our branch is pretty small. Technically I'm the youth services librarian—children and teens— but we all kind of pitch in with a little bit of everything around here. Did the county fill you in on any of that when they hired you?"

Cass shook her head. "I think it just said assistant librarian on the job offer. But this is the fourth library system I've worked in, so I know they're all different. I figured I'd go where you guys need me."

"Fourth?" Darcy repeated with a cocked eyebrow. "Not that I'm surprised, really. I know most people don't get what they want at their first job. Very few people seem to *choose* to be a children's librarian, for example. Everyone wants to be an archivist," she said, a note of mild disapproval in her voice.

Cass smirked. "That is the dream job."

"I'm the odd one out," said Darcy. "If I had it my way, youth services is all I'd do. It's much more my style than the other work we have to do here. Too bad Douglas County's budget is next to nonexistent."

"You could probably get a job at a bigger system," Cass suggested. "Children's librarians who actually *want* to be children's librarians are a hot commodity. If a library knew you'd stay with them, they'd probably hire you in a heartbeat."

Darcy shrugged, avoiding Cass's gaze. "Yeah, I know. It would just be hard for me to leave Riddle, you know what I mean?"

Cass took a sip of her mud-coffee to keep herself from making a face. Why anyone would *choose* to stay in a backwater town like this—especially when she had good job prospects somewhere else, even somewhere reasonably close like Medford or Eugene—was beyond her ability to fathom.

The next hour was spent introducing Cass to the ins and outs of the library. There wasn't a lot to learn; Cass had worked at so many libraries at this point that even though they were all different, she was able to find overlap of one aspect or another from her past experiences. On top of that, the Riddle Branch Library was much smaller than any other library she'd worked at. There were less moving parts, so to speak. Soon Darcy had gotten her logged into the Douglas County system—which used the same software as the second-to-last system Cass had worked at, so she only needed a slight refresher—and set her to work processing the small stack of returns from the previous Saturday, plus the ones that had been left in the dropbox on Sunday.

"While you work on that, I can start getting things together for our event today," Darcy said.

"Event?" Cass repeated.

"The summer scavenger hunt winners party. I hid some items around town this summer. The kids who found them all get to come this afternoon for a party. You know, lemonade, cookies, a little goody bag. That kind of thing."

"The brown-and-white dog," Cass said, mentally connecting the dots.

"You found the clue at the grocery store!" Darcy beamed. "I know it's not the flashiest of activities, but it was something easy enough to do and affordable on our budget. I wanted to do something extra besides the usual summer reading program. Get the kids out of the house and into the community."

"I think it was a great idea," Cass said with a smile. "Do you need help setting up for the party?"

"No, I think I'm good," Darcy replied. "If you could handle the desk, that'll free me up for the stuff I need to do." She let out a sigh, grinning. "It's such a relief to have someone else here. I know we're a small branch, but it's still too much work for just one person. Maybe now I can focus on doing more kids programming than just boring old homework hour."

Cass smiled stiffly. Now probably wouldn't be a good time to mention that she wasn't planning on sticking around long. Darcy was so excited, Cass didn't have the heart to burst her balloon so soon. She'd have to at some point, but there was no harm letting her be happy for a day. Darcy was so cheerful and enthusiastic, Cass couldn't help but like her already.

As Darcy had indicated, the library was not busy first thing in the morning. A few older patrons had wandered in, most heading for the computers or the periodicals. Only one came to the desk to ask Cass to check a book out for him, eschewing the self-checkout system. Cass was able to quickly get the stack of books checked back in and placed on the shelving cart.

She was just debating whether she should leave her post at the front desk—not like she wouldn't notice if someone needed help while she was restocking, considering how small the building was— when the glass doors at the front swung open. She glanced up, her eyes widening slightly in surprise.

It was the girl. Tom Kowalski's daughter. Possibly the figure she'd seen in the woods her first day in Riddle.

And definitely the girl from her dream last night.

The girl stopped in her tracks at the sight of Cass behind the front desk. They stared at each other for a moment before Cass found her voice and asked, "Can I help you?"

The girl looked down at her feet. "Um, is Ms. Hudson not working today?"

"I'm back here, Lily!" Darcy called before Cass could respond. The girl's face lit up at the sound of her voice. She started forward, then glanced at Cass. "Um, excuse me," she murmured before scooting between two rows of bookcases and disappearing into the children's corner.

Cass could hear them talking a little from her post at the front desk. Lily must be a frequent patron of the library, because she and Darcy seemed to have an easy rapport. The little girl asked Darcy if there was anything she could help with for the party, and Darcy told her she could tape up the stack of paper decorations she'd brought.

Finally, after a few minutes' quiet, Cass decided to leave her post and took the shelving cart over to the stacks. From where she stood, she could see Darcy tying off cellophane prize bags while Lily diligently pulled strips of masking tape and rolled them, placing them on the back of paper printouts of cartoon characters that Darcy had cut out. Tying off one last bag, Darcy looked up and caught Cass's eye over the top of the shelves.

"You're doing a great job. I'll be right back," Darcy said to Lily before leaving the children's corner to come over to where Cass stood.

"She's been here almost every day this summer," Darcy explained in a low voice. "I've been letting her help out just to keep her occupied. She's a really sweet girl, very sensitive, and I don't think she gets a lot of attention at home, if you know what I mean."

Cass frowned. "I think I met her yesterday, sort of. She was with her dad. He owns the property north of my aunt's. He came over to"—she paused, not wanting to go into too much detail—"introduce himself."

Darcy's eyes widened a little. "That's right! Is it true you're living in the Russo house? I mean, I saw your last name on the staff list, but I wasn't a hundred percent sure."

"Yeah, Alexandra Russo was my great-aunt," Cass said. "You call it the Russo house?" She chuckled wryly at the thought. A name like that made it sound like something out of a horror movie. Although, based on the things that had been happening since Cass arrived, maybe that wasn't that far off base.

Darcy nodded. "Technically, it's listed in the registry of historical places as the Porter house, but Alexandra Russo owned it for so long that we've all been calling it that for years." She paused. "Mr. Kowalski... he didn't say anything to you about buying it, did he?"

Cass shifted uncomfortably, turning back to the shelving cart. Why was everyone around here so obsessed with what she was going to do with that house?

"I'm sorry, it's none of my business," Darcy said quickly. "I didn't mean to pry."

"It's okay," Cass said with a shrug.

"It's just..." Darcy turned to the children's corner, where Lily was sticking more tape on the back of a paper cutout. She didn't appear to be listening, but Darcy frowned and ushered Cass further into the stacks. "It's just that Mr. Kowalski... hasn't lived in Riddle for very long. And he's not... necessarily... particularly popular among the people who live here. Don't get me wrong!" she added quickly when Cass rolled her eyes. "I know what you're thinking—typical small-town resistance to newcomers. But it really isn't that, Cass, honestly. It's... it's just *him*."

Cass felt a ripple down her back, and she stiffened. That feeling again. "What about *him*?" she asked.

Darcy began to pick at the sleeve of her cardigan. This must be a habit of hers, Cass realized, because there was a hole worn into the cuff. "He started off on the wrong foot as soon as he got here. My dad's on the board at the chamber of commerce. Their meetings are open to the public, and they have this thing where if you want to have the floor, you throw a buck in the jar." She colored at Cass's quirked eyebrow and quickly explained, "That helps fund the programs they do in the community, it's not just a money grab. Anyway, they'll usually wind up with, like, ten or fifteen bucks per meeting at the most. But right after Mr. Kowalski moved here, he went to the meeting and sat there for most of it without saying anything. Then at the end, when they asked if there was any more business before they adjourned, he stood up and he threw a *hundred dollar bill* in the jar. And he said, 'Starting today, things are going to change around here.'"

Cass's jaw dropped. "Seriously?" Any charitable feelings she'd been beginning to have toward him vanished. What sort of person would move to a new town and tell the residents that he was going to *change* their home? His ego must be a force of nature.

Darcy nodded. "It put a lot of people's backs up. Riddle isn't"— she frowned, seeming to struggle to come up with the right way to phrase it—"as prosperous as it used to be. Hasn't been for years, not since the tin mine closed and our government betters decimated the timber industry. But we're a tight-knit town. We're a community. Some stranger coming in and saying he wants to change everything..."

"Yeah," Cass said, exhaling and looking back over in the direction of the children's corner. "I've never been much of a *community* person, but even I can see how that would tick people off." She glanced back at Darcy. "But what does that have to do with my aunt's—my—property?"

"He's been trying to get his hands on that land for as long as he's been here," Darcy said. "He's a real estate developer. He's got stuff going up all over the county. High-end housing developments. You know, the ones with a giant house on a tiny lot that sells for half a million dollars. He's had plans drawn up for what he'd do to your aunt's property for a long time now. With that many acres, he could probably cram in five or six hundred houses."

Cass choked on nothing again. "Five or six *hundred?*" she spurted. "He's insane! This town already only has a thousand people living in it. Where does he think he's going to get the people to buy the houses?"

"He markets to Californians. That's where he came from originally, apparently. He's hoping to get people who are relocating, retiring to Oregon to get away from the cost of living down there. There's quite a bit of that going on right now."

Cass shook her head. "I can't believe *that* many people would want to come *here*. I mean—" She broke off, not sure if her words would be offensive to Darcy.

"No, it's okay," Darcy said with a shrug. "I know what you mean. It's in the middle of nowhere. But there's the casino nearby, and Crater Lake not far off, and there've been so many new vineyards and wineries and craft breweries opening up. He thinks there's a possibility to transform Riddle into a *destination*. But..." She trailed off, silent for a moment before finally saying, quietly, "It would be quite a transformation for the people who live here."

Cass remembered the way Darcy had said she didn't want to

leave Riddle earlier, an odd sensation tugging at her heartstrings. It was difficult for Cass to imagine anyone being so tied to one place that they'd feel so strongly about it. But Darcy's feelings were clear on her face. She loved this town. She was protective of it.

"Wouldn't the city council have to approve that?" Cass asked.

Darcy smirked. "Hey, money talks. And Mr. Kowalski has a lot of money. Besides, the idea of Riddle becoming more… upscale, I guess, has appeal to a lot of people. Not everyone. But the people on the city council, anyway. After all, think of all that extra money from property taxes." She sighed. "Besides, as they're constantly reminding us, there's a housing shortage in Oregon. People are coming here from all over the place. They have to go somewhere. The house prices have been driven up so much they're barely affordable for regular Oregonians."

"Yeah, but how does building houses with a starting price point of half a million dollars address that?"

Darcy shrugged but didn't answer, instead taking a book off the shelving cart and turning it over in her hands. "I'd better go finish setting up." She set the book back down before looking at Cass. "Don't take it out on Lily, though, huh? She's a good kid. She has nothing to do with any of this. She's already got it rough enough without people in town taking the circumstances of her birth out on her."

"Do people do that?" Cass asked.

Darcy nodded grimly, her mouth a thin line, before leaving

Cass alone with the shelving cart and her thoughts.

Cass sighed. She didn't like this. But what was she supposed to do about it? Even if she didn't sell to Kowalski, what was to prevent whomever wound up buying the house from turning around and selling it to him two months later, anyway? This was out of her hands. What happened to Riddle was not her problem. Like Darcy said, this was happening all over Oregon—all over the country, honestly. There was no sense getting worked up about it. She couldn't change it.

From the children's corner, she could hear the sound of Lily's voice, asking a question of Darcy that Cass couldn't quite make out. She felt for the girl, too, if what Darcy said about the way people in town treated her was true. No wonder she spent so much time at the library.

But that got Cass wondering—what did she do with the rest of her time? Wander the woods around Alexandra's house, maybe? It would make sense, especially if she didn't have a lot of friends. Cass probably would have done the same thing at that age if her Sight hadn't made her avoid all greenbelts like the plague. She wondered for a brief moment what her own childhood would have been like if she'd been normal, if seeing things no one else could see hadn't gotten her labeled a freak so early on. But Cass couldn't really picture herself ever having been Miss Popularity, Sight or no. She wasn't cut out for fitting in. One more thing she and Lily had in common.

She pulled another book off the shelving cart, kneeling on the floor to replace it on a lower shelf. Now more than ever, Cass was convinced Lily was the one she'd seen in the woods yesterday. But had she been the one who left the tarot card for Cass to find? If so, why?

And if not Lily... then who?

Chapter 6

Darcy took her lunch early, so as to be back in time for the children's party at one o'clock. "Are you sure you'll be all right?" she asked Cass, withdrawing her purse from the cubby behind the front desk where they'd both stowed their belongings this morning and rummaging through it for her keys.

"No problem," Cass said. There were only a few patrons in the library at the moment—a couple people sitting at the computers, an older man reading a newspaper, a woman browsing the romance section, and Lily, still sitting quietly in the children's corner.

"Right," Darcy said, pulling out a set of keys with a pink plush bear keychain attached to them. "I'll be back in a jiffy, then."

Darcy hurried out the front door, leaving Cass sitting at the desk. Cass sighed. First weeks were always the hardest; she was sure there were things that needed doing, but Darcy hadn't had time to give her much training today, so apart from shelving and checking patrons out, there wasn't a lot for Cass to do with herself.

Eventually the woman browsing the romance section came to the front, giving Cass an awkward smile before bringing her stack of books to the self-checkout kiosk. Cass watched her for a moment before letting out a sigh and getting to her feet. Maybe there were some shelves in need of tidying.

She walked up and down the rows of shelves, looking for any books that seemed out of place, straightening books that had been set back crookedly and righting a handful that some wiseacre had stuck back on the shelf pages-out, spine-in. When she made it to the children's corner, she chanced a glance over at Lily Kowalski, who was sitting at one of the tables with a piece of paper and a box of colored crayons. Open in front of her was a large hardcover book with full-page illustrations. Cass paused, looking more carefully at the book. She recognized it: *Faeries* by Brian Froud. Aunt Alexandra had given her a copy when she was young so she could learn the names of the different species of fae she encountered. Lily had the book open to an illustration of a pixy crouching on a mushroom cap. It appeared Lily was using the painting as a model for her own drawing, but her picture looked different. Even from this distance, it was familiar to Cass.

Before Cass could move away, the girl glanced up from her drawing, catching Cass's eye. Cass smiled awkwardly. "Hey," she said. "You like faeries?"

The little girl flushed. "Yeah," she murmured. "I guess." She moved her arm, covering the drawing.

Cass smiled again and turned away. She could be wrong, but... she could have sworn she recognized the creature Lily was drawing.

One with pointy features and a green face.

Darcy came racing back through the library doors at five minutes to one, shoveling the last of a burger and a handful of fries into her mouth.

"It's a good thing you made it," Cass said in a tight, low voice as Darcy practically hurled her purse back into its cubby. "There are a lot of kids back there, and I have no clue what to do with them." When the first few kids had come in, she'd sent them automatically to the children's corner, but she'd quickly realized that was a mistake. Unfortunately, by then the damage had already been done. Darcy hadn't been kidding when she said that Lily was not the most popular girl in town. She'd still been working on her drawing when the first two kids, a sister and brother who appeared to be twins, had arrived for the party. Though she'd quickly thrown her arm over the top of it the way she had when she'd noticed Cass looking, she hadn't been fast enough to distract the other children.

"Drawing more of your imaginary friends?" the boy had asked, a sneer audible in his voice.

"No," Lily had replied softly. "I just thought the pictures in this book were pretty."

"Prettier than what you could draw, I'm sure," the girl had said, picking up the Brian Froud book and flipping through it. "Oh, *ew!*" she'd cried, aghast. "They're all *naked!*"

"Not all of them," Lily had quietly protested, her face beet red.

But the siblings paid no mind. The boy had quickly snatched the book out of his sister's hands and begun gawking at one of the more sensual of the painted fae. "Gross," he'd said after a moment, as if to justify himself.

Cass had rolled her eyes. *Yeah, I'll just* bet *it's gross. That's why you can't look away, huh, kid?* Meanwhile, Lily had wordlessly crumpled her drawing into her fist and stood up. She'd walked over to the blue recycling bin next to the front desk, avoiding Cass's eyes as she tossed her drawing inside. Another group of kids came through the doors then, pushing past Lily without so much as a glance and hurrying to the children's corner to join the twins in gawking at the Froud book. Lily had trudged back over and grabbed her backpack, moving to the table farthest away from the other kids, and that's where she still sat when Darcy burst back in.

"Okay, all set," Darcy said now, whirling away from the desk.

"Not quite," Cass said, gesturing with her finger to her chin.

"Oh!" Darcy cried, hurrying back to her purse to grab a tissue to wipe her face with. "And you'd better take your lunch, too."

"Uh," Cass said, glancing at the noisy crowd of kids in the

children's corner, "shouldn't I stay to assist any patrons that come in while you're busy with that?"

Darcy waved her off. "No, no, it's fine. The last thing I need is to get in trouble with Randy for not giving you your state-mandated lunch on time. Once I get them started on their crafts, I can leave them if someone comes in."

Cass found herself staring at Lily again. She knew the kids would lay off her when Darcy was back there, but as soon as Darcy left them unsupervised it would start again. But there was nothing she could do about it. She didn't know this girl from a load of hay, anyway.

Still, she couldn't help the way her heart had gone out to Lily when that kid had taunted her about her *"imaginary friends."* Cass had heard that sentence so many times as a child that she'd lost count. But did it mean the same thing to Lily as it had to Cass? It could just be a coincidence, but the drawing had Cass wondering if maybe there was another reason Lily had been poking around the woods besides just childish boredom.

As Darcy bustled back to the children's corner, Cass surreptitiously stooped, withdrawing the crumpled drawing from the recycling bin. She wanted to get a better look at it to see if her suspicions had been correct—but not here, where Lily or the other kids might see. She tucked the paper into her pocket and then grabbed her purse and lunch from the cubby behind the desk. Not knowing where the fast food restaurants around here were to be found, she had packed a lunch for herself in a brown paper sack. But she wasn't going to eat it in here, with all the kids and the noise. It was a sunny day, and she'd seen upon arriving this morning that the Riddle City Park sprawled along next to the library building. There were sure to be some picnic tables she could sit at to eat her lunch.

She left the library, looking around. To the east of the library stood the police station and, across a small stub street, the town community center. Further to the south were a set of tennis courts, and then, uncomfortably close to the courts, the town's wastewater treatment plant. Cass decided to go west, moving away from the plant along a trail that bisected the park's green grass. At the end of the path she could see a body of water, and as she drew closer, she saw a sign indicating that this was Cow Creek. A running trail snaked along parallel to the banks of the creek, and a few worn benches were bolted to the ground beside it. She sank onto one, setting her purse and bag lunch on the seat beside her. She breathed out, closing her eyes and enjoying the moment of quiet... Or, mostly quiet. Just audible over the burble of the running water was the light, tinkling sound of laughter—laughter of the non-human variety. A pair of water sprites were playing in the creek not far from where Cass was sitting. She sighed and opened her eyes, reaching for the paper sack. There really was no escaping these things here, was there?

She took a bite out of the peanut butter-and-jelly (jam, rather—

she'd found a jar of Alexandra's homemade blackberry jam in the pantry this morning, still sealed from the last time Alexandra had canned, which, according to the label on the jar, had been last summer) sandwich she'd made this morning. The jam tasted good, fresh and sweet. She took another bite, chewing thoughtfully as she fumbled to pull the crumpled drawing out of her pocket with her right hand while holding the sandwich in her left. As she smoothed the drawing out on her lap, she heard the sound of approaching footsteps accompanied by the sound of jingling tags. Just someone walking their dog. She paid no attention, looking instead down at the paper in her lap. Lily was a good artist for her age. And this drawing—she definitely hadn't imagined it earlier. It really did look like the green thing she'd been seeing all around Alexandra's property. The fae creature that somehow, impossibly, had been able to talk to her...

"No MoonPies today?" a voice asked.

Cass's head jerked up at the sound. The dog-walker had stopped about five feet away from her, and she realized with a start that it was none other than the honey-haired man from the grocery store. He was wearing a gray cotton T-shirt and jeans. Beside him on a leash, a red Doberman with floppy ears wagged its stub of a tail.

She felt her face start to blaze at the sight of him, but she tried to play it off cool. "Oh, uh, no," she said after a moment, once her brain caught up with her and she realized he'd asked her a question.

"Not today. Just a boring old peanut butter sandwich." She smiled with her mouth closed, surreptitiously running her tongue over her teeth and hoping that she hadn't flashed him a chunk of blackberry when she'd spoken.

"Nothing wrong with the classics," he said with a grin. "I wasn't sure if I'd run into you again. Are you new in town?"

"Oh, yeah," Cass responded once her innards had finished melting at the sight of that grin. *Honestly, Cass, will you get it together?* "Well, sort of. My great-aunt lived here and she recently passed, so I'm staying at her place for the time being while I sort out her affairs."

His grin faded at her words. "I'm so sorry for your loss," he said sincerely.

"Thank you," said Cass.

"I'm Matthew, by the way. Matthew McCarthy." He gestured to the Doberman, who had come up to Cass and was staring intently at the crust of her sandwich. "And this idiot is Tucker."

Cass let out a little gasp of mock offense. "Who are you calling an idiot?" she said, reaching out to stroke the dog's ears. They were soft and silky. Tucker, for his part, looked at her with mournful brown eyes, the disappointment that she was merely offering him pets and not her sandwich written all over his face.

"I call him what I know him to be," Matthew said solemnly. At Cass's snort, he grinned and added, "Most people are afraid of Dobermans because of their size, but I learned a while ago that most of them don't realize just how big they are. This guy seems to believe he's approximately the size of a Dachshund, which means that he cowers before animals half his size and thinks he should be allowed to sit in my lap." Cass laughed, and Tucker's stub tail began to wag even harder.

"Quite the masterpiece you have there," Matthew said after a moment. Cass looked at him in confusion before realizing that he was staring at Lily's drawing, which she'd set down on the bench in order to pet Tucker. "Did you draw it yourself?"

Cass laughed. "I'm not half so talented. No, Lily Kowalski— uh, that is, a little girl at the library drew it. That's where I work, for now," she explained, her face flushing again at his warm brown eyes on hers. "She threw it away, but it seemed like a shame."

"Lily Kowalski, huh?" He looked down at the drawing again. "Good to know I'll have at least one talented artist. That'll make projects fun. I'm a fourth grade teacher and she's going to be in my class starting next week," he explained.

"Oh," Cass said. So he was a schoolteacher. For some reason, this made her remember her dream, in which he'd been reading, and her face grew hot again. "How long have you taught at Riddle Elementary?"

"This is going to be my first year. Yup," he said, grinning at her expression, "you're not the only newcomer in town. I was with 4J— uh, Eugene School District, that is—for a few years, but I decided it was time for a change."

"What made you pick *Riddle* of all places?" Cass asked in surprise.

Matthew shrugged, not meeting her eyes. "I don't know," he said. "I just had a feeling this was where I was meant to go."

She quirked her head at him, but before he could elaborate, Tucker took advantage of their distraction and with one swift motion of his long snoot, grabbed the rest of her sandwich out of her hand.

"Tucker!" Matthew scolded, pulling the dog back by his leash, but it was too late. "I am so sorry!"

Cass just laughed, waving him off. "It's fine. I have another half, and anyway, it was just the crust. I would have offered it to him, but I wasn't sure if he'd be allowed to have it."

"He does have a weakness for peanut butter," Matthew said in a long-suffering way. "Well, I'll let you get back to your lunch. It was nice talking to you, uh—"

Cass flushed as she realized she hadn't introduced herself. Once again, she had the slightly-overwhelmed feeling of being around an insanely attractive guy and consequently making a fool out of herself. "It's Cass," she said, twisting the key around her neck awkwardly. "Cass Russo."

"Nice to meet you, Cass," Matthew said with a warm smile. "I'll see you around."

"Yeah, see you. Bye, Tucker," she said as Matthew guided the dog away from her.

She watched them as they started down the path that bisected the park toward the library. Her eyebrows rose as she noticed that there was a mass market paperback sticking out of the back pocket of his jeans. (Okay, yes, she was looking at his butt. She couldn't help it! Everything about that man seemed to have been forged by the gods.)

But it wasn't the book or even his butt that made Cass's eyes widen. It was the words printed on the book's cover: *The Lion, The Witch and The Wardrobe.* She hadn't remembered until that very second, seeing it again right in front of her face, but she was sure of it. She knew she was remembering right.

That was the book he'd been reading in the dream.

Chapter 7

"You had a naughty dream about the guy from the grocery store?"

Emma was laughing at her. She wasn't even trying to conceal it. The line crackled with static from the volume of her howls.

Cass felt her face burning all over again. "It wasn't a *naughty* dream," she said, her voice at a whisper even though she was in the privacy of her own house. Well, Aunt Alexandra's house. Not that Alexandra was there to hear it. But Cass *felt* like she was, like she could hear everything, and her embarrassment was supreme.

"It sounds like it was a naughty dream."

"It wasn't!"

"You dreamed he was in your bed."

"Yeah, but we weren't doing anything. He was just... *there*. In my room."

Emma snorted again. "Why're you so embarrassed, then? You're thirty years old, Cass. I think I had racier dreams than that when I was twelve."

"Because he's a stranger!" Cass hissed, still whispering. "And because I dreamed we were... married, I guess."

"*Married?*" Emma's laughter stopped.

Cass shrugged uncomfortably. "I dunno. It felt that way. Maybe because of the little girl." And the strong maternal instincts she'd felt toward her as they'd walked through the woods together. The way she'd thought she was *theirs*. And those feelings hadn't started when the girl had shown up, they'd been there through the whole dream. The dream had been more than just a make-out dream with the grocery store guy—Matthew, she remembered with another agonizing flush, Matthew McCarthy, fourth grade teacher—it had been the *feelings*. The familiarity. It hadn't *felt* like just a dream, it had been like... a glimpse into another life. A life of shared history, of memories that she couldn't access but knew were there. Of trust built over time. That's what had made the dream so intense. So mortifying.

Almost worse than if it *had* just been a naughty dream.

"Maybe it was a premonition," Emma suggested, her voice suddenly serious.

"No!" Cass cried, her voice jumping from hushed to shrill.

"Well, it's not like you to dream you're *married* to some guy you met for thirty seconds at the grocery store. But it *is* like you to have dreams about the future..."

"That's not my future," Cass said firmly. She knew it couldn't be. She'd given up on that kind of future. Shoved it in a box and locked it away. A future like that could never work out, not for someone like her. She'd learned that the hard way. "Anyway, that wasn't the part of the dream I called you about and you know it. It was that other part."

"The 'we're all going to die' part?" Emma asked. "Yeah, that is a little more troubling, I suppose."

"You think?"

As she spoke, she heard a noise from over her head. A dull *thunk*, like something falling over in the room upstairs. She sighed wearily. There was a chance, she supposed, that Onyx could have knocked something over—he did seem to be the sort of cat who enjoyed the "knock everything off your nightstand and dresser at three in the morning until you wake up screaming" game—but she had a feeling that he was not the culprit.

"Hang on," she said to Emma. "I'm going to have to call you back."

"What? No!" Emma protested, but Cass barely heard her distant voice as she moved the phone away from her ear. "Don't you dare hang up on me! I'm not done with you yet!"

"Talk to you later," Cass said, pressing the *end* button and shoving the phone into her back pocket. She looked around the kitchen for something to arm herself with. It needed to be iron, but did Alexandra have any iron in the house? Considering the brownie she'd seen inside on the first day, she was disinclined to think so. Finally, after rummaging through enough cupboards, she encountered a cast-iron skillet. Did cast-iron count? It was probably the best she was going to get. Brandishing the skillet, Cass went upstairs.

The second-floor hallway was dim, lit only by the sunlight streaming in from the transoms and through Cass's open bedroom door. But something about the hall looked odd to her. Finally, she realized what it was—there was light coming from the end of the hall where the door to the servants' stairs was located. She was certain that that door had been locked when she checked it the first day she'd been in Riddle, but she hadn't checked it again. Now the door was open. She swallowed, trying to ignore the prickles she felt running across her skin. She tightened her grip on the skillet and moved down the hall.

Sure enough, the door to the servants' staircase was now open. Through the door was a small landing between the steps leading down and those going up to the finished attic where the old servants' quarters were located. If Cass remembered correctly, Aunt Alexandra had used those rooms for storage, since that floor was far too warm most of the year to be livable (unless, you know, you're a servant; then your comfort doesn't matter, apparently). The landing was lit by a square window with plain, clear glass. The late afternoon sunlight streamed in from the west with an odd green tint due to the leaves on the tree directly outside it.

Cass looked around, wondering what could have caused the

thump she'd heard from downstairs. She didn't see anything that could have been knocked over; the landing was devoid of any furniture or knickknacks. Maybe the door had been stuck, and the *thunk* was the sound it made when… someone had managed to pry it open?

The question was who—or what—had done it. She looked all around but didn't see or hear anything that indicated the presence of fae in the space. But what else could it have been? There was no such thing as ghosts…

Cass froze, thinking that over. There *was* no such thing as ghosts, right? She'd never seen one, and you'd think that if she could see fae, she'd be able to see ghosts. But what if she was wrong? What if her Sight was only honed to one aspect of the paranormal, but there were others she didn't know about?

She suddenly felt very alarmed. She started to turn to leave the landing, but two things happened to stop her: First, out of the corner of her eye, she caught a familiar flash of color. Her subconscious registered it as yet another tarot card, lying askew on one of the steps leading up to the attic.

At the same time, there was a loud *thunk* against the glass of the square window. She jumped, an involuntary half-gasp, half-strangled-scream tearing out of her throat. What had that been? A bird hitting the window?

She grabbed the tarot card off the steps, shoving it in her back pocket without looking at it, and went to the window, peering out.

Then she groaned. Not a bird. That green fae thing was back, sitting in the branches of the tree just outside. When she appeared at the window, it dropped the acorn it was holding—the previous *thunk* must have been the sound of another acorn hitting the glass as it tried to get her attention—and waved at her.

She shoved up the sash and stuck her head out the window. "What do you want?"

The creature didn't respond, but it pointed down into the side yard of the house. Cass followed its gesture with her eyes and her brows rose. Through the branches of the tree she could just see a girl sitting on the wooden bench in the small side garden. Cass recognized her immediately. It was Lily Kowalski.

She didn't hesitate to ask why the creature wanted Cass to see her. She suspected, at this point, that she knew. But she had to make sure. She quickly shoved the window closed, twisting the brass lock into place, and hurried back into the hallway. She didn't know whether the door at the bottom of the servants' stairs would be locked or stuck—she knew that the door was in the kitchen, but just like with the upstairs door, she hadn't messed around with it when it didn't immediately open on the first day—so she ran back to the main staircase, down into the foyer, and out the front door.

When she got down the front porch steps, she paused to catch her breath. She didn't want to scare the girl by running up to her like a hyperventilating maniac wielding a cast-iron skillet. She set the skillet down on the bottom step and ran a hand through her dark hair to smooth it. Then she walked casually around the side of the house.

What she saw when she made her way down the slope into the garden made her brows rise once again. Sitting beside Lily on the bench was a squat gnome, its skin mottled like bark on a tree, its head wide and flat on top like a mushroom cap. It was weaving a cat's cradle out of a gossamer spider web. Lily sat facing the creature with her hands raised, silver webbing dangling from the tips of her two index fingers. The gnome laughed, a sound not unlike the chattering of a chipmunk, as the two of them adjusted the pattern of the cat's cradle.

Lily was *playing* with it.

Cass exhaled. That answered that question—Lily could definitely see fae, then. Her drawing in the library hadn't been a coincidence. So much about this enigma of a child suddenly made sense. Cass remembered the way the other kids had teased Lily for her "imaginary friends" earlier. Her parentage wasn't the only reason the other children of Riddle were giving Lily a wide berth. Cass couldn't blame Lily for having shared her secret, whether accidentally or by design; Cass had made the same mistake as a kid, not realizing that others couldn't see the same things she could or that most people didn't believe in things like faeries and magic. It had only taken a couple slip-ups to get her labeled a pariah, a reputation she hadn't been able to shake until her parents had finally packed up and moved from that town when she was eleven, transplanting the family to Chicago, where she'd met Emma. But what Cass didn't understand was why, after all the trouble they'd clearly caused her, Lily was still deliberately seeking the fae out rather than steering as far away from them as possible.

Apparently *seeing* and *having common sense about* didn't go hand-in-hand.

"Hey, Lily," she said as she approached the bench. Lily looked up, and the gnome dropped the cobwebs, skittering away and chattering all the while.

"Wait, come back!" Lily cried as the gnome disappeared into the bushes. "She's a friend! She won't hurt you!"

Cass smirked to herself. *I wouldn't be so sure about that*, she thought wryly. Word of her eviction of the brownie must have been going around, based on the scowl the gnome was giving her from between the curling branches of a fern.

"So," Cass said, sitting on the bench beside Lily in the spot vacated by the gnome. The seat was still warm, she noticed with a frown. "What are you doing here, exactly?"

"I'm sorry, ma'am," Lily said, doing that thing that only kids seem to be able to accomplish, sitting up straight and slouching at the same time, with her hands on her knees and her arms ramrod straight. Her face was red, and she didn't quite look Cass in the eye. Cass tried not to let the "ma'am" bug her. She supposed that, to a nine-year-old, all adults were *ma'am*s. "I know you said this was private property. I just... I didn't know where else to go. I always used to come here in the summer, before. My friends live here."

"Your... friends?"

"Yeah. Like the gnome who was just here. And Mr. Green."

Cass's brow furrowed. "Who's Mr. Green?"

"You really don't know?"

The response hadn't come from Lily, but from a familiar high-pitched voice over her left shoulder. She turned to see the green fae, who had come down from the tree's high branches and was sitting on a paving stone at the edge of the garden, watching Cass and the girl.

"Mr. Green!" Lily cried in delight. "There you are! I haven't seen you in a week. I was starting to get worried!"

"I've been busy keeping track of this interloper," the creature said, narrowing its eyes at Cass, a hint of mischief in its voice. She frowned. What did it mean by *keeping track* of her?

"Your name is Mr. Green?" she asked aloud.

"I don't have a name," the creature responded shirtily. "Names are human inventions."

Cass rolled her eyes. Fae *did*, in fact, have names, at least according to Aunt Alexandra—but to know a fae's true name was to have power over it, so surely the creature wouldn't want humans to know about it.

The fae hopped across the path almost like a frog, but it stayed well out of arm's reach. It leveled a gaze at Cass. "But some humans have called me Green," it said after a long moment.

Cass quirked her head. There was an odd, loaded tone to its words, and for some reason, they gave her a strong sense of... something. Not quite a premonition. More like déjà vu.

Before Cass could put her finger on the sensation, Lily asked, "What's an interloper?"

"An interloper," Green said cheerfully, pointing to Cass, "is what she is."

"Ah," Lily said, pretending to understand what the fae meant when she clearly hadn't.

"Do fae typically have genders?" Cass asked. Despite the imaginative—and *detailed*—drawings of Mr. Froud, she'd never seen any clear indication that any fae was male or female. From what she understood of them, fae didn't reproduce like animals. They seemed to spring into existence spontaneously, or through magic or something.

"More human inventions," Green confirmed. "But the little one calls everyone she meets Mister or Missus, so I told her Mister is fine."

"It's true," Lily said, nodding serenely. She was practically radiating happiness at having the weird creature near. Cass tried to hold back a sigh. She was going to have to do a lot of work with this kid.

"If you want, you can call me Mister, too. I sort of like the respect it adds," Green said with a sly grin.

"Lily," Cass said, ignoring the fae and trying to keep her voice even and patient, "did my aunt know that you could see faeries?"

"Ms. Alexandra? Oh, yes," Lily replied, beaming. "She was giving me lessons... before." At that, the joy seemed to drain out of her face, and her shoulders slumped. "I'm sorry for your loss, ma'am."

Cass frowned. It was obvious from Lily's reaction that she and Aunt Alexandra had been close. But why hadn't Alexandra ever mentioned Lily to Cass when they'd spoken on the phone? It seemed a striking omission.

"What sort of lessons?" she asked as Lily looked down at her feet. She was wearing saddle shoes. That was another odd thing about the girl, the old-fashioned, almost prissy way she dressed. While the other kids at the library wore jeans and sneakers, Cass had only ever seen Lily in skirts or jumpers. She wondered if the clothing was Lily's choice or her parents'.

"How to control my ability," Lily said softly, still seeming off in a world of her own. To Cass's surprise, Green moved closer, putting a small, spindly hand on Lily's shoe in an almost comforting gesture. Lily looked up at him and smiled.

"Your ability?" Cass asked.

"Yes, her ability. Do you have to repeat every other word we say?" Green said, looking at Cass in annoyance. "You know what *ability* means, right? You should, seeing as you have one yourself."

Cass stared between the fae and the girl. "You mean my premonitions?"

"Right," Green said. "Those."

Lily turned to face Cass eagerly. "You have one, too?"

"Yeah, I have premonitions. I mean... sometimes I can sense when something's going to happen," Cass explained. "Not always. But sometimes."

"That's sort of like me!" Lily exclaimed. "Sometimes I can hear what people think. But not always. Just sometimes."

Cass blinked at the girl. "You can *hear* people's *thoughts?*" Cass had never encountered anyone else with a supernatural ability apart from Aunt Alexandra, and her ability had been the same as Cass's. She hadn't realized that other abilities were even possible.

Lily nodded. "Ms. Alexandra was helping me learn how to control it. Sometimes I don't hear anything, but other times it's like..." She hesitated, her gaze on the gnome, who had reappeared from the bushes and was collecting empty acorn caps that lay strewn on the ground beneath the oak trees. "Other times it's like I have fifty people standing around me screaming in my ears. It gives me a headache."

"I can imagine," Cass said, frowning. She'd thought she had it bad, being the unwanted harbinger of doom, but at least she didn't have other people's voices in her head.

Lily sat quietly for a moment before saying, "Ma'am..."

"Cass."

Lily nodded. "Ms. Cass... do you think you would be able to give me lessons?"

Cass stared at the girl, her brows raised. "Me?"

"You know, since you also have an ability. I thought maybe…" Lily trailed off and shrugged.

There it was again, that same pang she'd felt in her chest when she'd watched Lily decorating for the party earlier, when Darcy said she'd spent most of her summer at the library. Had she been spending more time there because Alexandra was gone? Losing Alexandra was hard enough for Cass, even though she'd had her beloved great-aunt for thirty years. She couldn't imagine how she would have felt if Aunt Alexandra had passed when she was only nine. It must have been so hard for Lily, not only losing someone she cared about, but also the only other person she knew with the Sight.

Cass exhaled. *You're supposed to be avoiding attachments, remember?* she reminded herself. *How will Lily feel if she gets close to you and then you leave?*

Still, Cass was going to be here at least a few more months. And Lily clearly needed help. The last thing Cass wanted was for the girl to get spirited away because she hadn't had anyone to warn her, to help her know better. Cass remembered the way she—someone who had been practicing ignoring faery influences for half her life—had been pixy-led last week. No, these woods were definitely not safe for a little girl to be wandering around in alone, especially not a little girl with Sight. Cass would just have to make it clear to her that these lessons were *temporary*.

"Sure," Cass said after a long moment. When Lily let out a little squeal of glee, she quickly added, "Now, I can't make any promises about the *quality* of these lessons. I've never been a teacher, and I don't know nearly as much about this as Aunt Alexandra did."

"That's what you've got me for," Green said from where he sat on top of Lily's saddle shoe.

Cass narrowed her eyes at him. "I never said you were going to be part of it. In fact, if I have my way, you won't be anywhere near us."

"But Mr. Green always helped with my lessons with Ms. Alexandra!" Lily protested.

Cass's head jerked up at her. "Excuse me, *what?*"

Green folded his arms smugly and nodded.

Cass gaped at the two of them. What had happened to Aunt Alexandra over the last twenty years of her life? Letting brownies in the *house?* Giving lessons to some local kid without breathing a word of it to Cass any of the hundreds of times they'd talked on the phone? Befriending this... this... green *thing?* It was like she'd been living a double life!

She squeezed her eyes shut and reached for the key around her neck, twisting it between her fingers. Just now, she'd give anything, *anything,* to be able to talk to her great-aunt one last time. To get some answers to the dozens of questions that had piled up over the last week. But it was impossible. All she could do was look forward.

Lily was insistent that Alexandra had trusted Green. But could she be sure Lily wasn't somehow bewitched? True, she didn't *seem* bewitched. And, honestly, in the time she'd spent sitting on this bench with the two of them, Cass hadn't felt any prickles of foreboding. In fact, it was possibly the first time since she'd arrived in Riddle that she'd gone this long *without* getting the creepy-crawlies.

But still...

"I'll think about it," Cass said at last. "But in the meantime, I don't want you wandering around the woods here by yourself, okay? They're dangerous."

"I know," Lily said. "Mr. Green already warned me."

Just like he'd warned Cass when she was being pixy-led. Cass knew the fae was having the same thought—or, based on his behavior the other day, maybe even *reading* her thoughts—from the smug expression on his face.

"Okay, then. Well, let's head inside and we can figure out where to go from here," Cass said.

"Mr. Green can't go in the house. Can we go in the solarium? That's where Ms. Alexandra and I would always go for lessons."

"All right," Cass said, wondering just how she'd managed to get mixed up in this mess. "You go ahead, I need to get some things together." Like books or something. Aunt Alexandra was bound to have some books or notes related to Lily's magic lessons, right? Somewhere in that labyrinthine house of hers.

Lily nodded, scrambling off the bench and bounding down the path to the south side of the house. As Cass watched her, Green let out a snort of laughter. "You have no clue what you're doing, do you?"

"Nope." She looked down at the fae. "Why do you care about any of this?"

Green shrugged. "Gives me something to do. You'd be surprised how tedious living forever can be. Gathering acorns gets dull after the first ten centuries or so. Even playing tricks on humans gets old when you've been around as long as me."

"So you decided to study the humans rather than just conducting random experiments on them?" Cass said. "You're what you might call a faery academic?"

The fae shrugged again. "I'm me."

"Right. You. *Green.*" Cass frowned at that déjà vu feeling she had once more when she said the creature's so-called name. "Are you the one who opened the door to the staircase earlier?"

"No. Lily told you, I don't go inside the house," Green replied in his high, lilting voice.

"Don't or can't?"

Green rolled his eyes, an oddly human gesture. "Only household fae go indoors. Brownies and the like." He wrinkled his nose, then added, "You're not too popular around here for kicking the brownies out, by the way."

Cass ignored him. Instead, she drew the tarot card she'd found on the servant stairs earlier out of her pocket. She hadn't had a chance to look at it before, but now she noticed that the image depicted a hand emerging from clouds holding a golden goblet. A white dove flew overhead, carrying in its beak what appeared to be a Eucharistic host. Bizarrely religious imagery, Cass remarked to herself, for something typically associated with the occult.

"So you're not the one who's been leaving these around for me?" she asked Green.

He looked at the card for a moment before saying blandly, "If I were to leave you a card, it certainly wouldn't be *that* one."

Cass blinked. "What's that supposed to mean?"

"I don't know. You tell me, if you're supposed to be so smart."

Cass groaned, biting the inside of her cheek. Twenty minutes in this fae's company was already driving her up the wall. How was she supposed to put up with him on a daily basis? Part of her wanted to tell Lily right now that she'd changed her mind, but she knew it wouldn't be that simple. Green would continue to harass her as long as she was here on Aunt Alexandra's property. What she needed to do was get the house cleared out as quickly as possible, and then get the heck out of this town before the residents—human or non-human—managed to strip her of her last vestige of sanity.

She put the tarot card back in her pocket, making a mental note to ask Emma about it later. For now, Lily was beckoning to her from the steps of the solarium. Whatever the mystery about these cards was, it would have to wait to be solved until another day.

Chapter 8

The next couple weeks went by in a blur. Lily came over to the house almost every day for her lessons—such as they were. Cass had found a few books in Alexandra's collection that had some information on the subject of preternatural abilities, including one called *Faery Blessings*, the title of which made Cass's eyes roll so hard they disappeared into her skull. As if her premonitions could be considered a blessing. *Faery Curses*, maybe.

The book had explained that gifts like Lily's were typically found in people with highly empathetic personalities. The more sensitive the possessor of the gift was to the feelings of others, the stronger the gift typically was, to the point that the feelings of others could sometimes be overwhelming to the possessor of the gift.

Out of curiosity, Cass had looked up premonitions. According to the book, prophecy was typically given to people with controlling personalities. Well, more specifically, *"someone who strongly desires to feel control over their situation."* Yeah, right. If anything, her premonitions had typically given Cass *less* control, since it seemed there was rarely anything she could *do* about it. When she warned people, they universally ignored her. To sometimes devastating results, Cass remembered grimly.

The book was a crock, she decided. But regardless, there was logic to the assumption that Lily would be able to control her powers better by improving her own self-confidence. Becoming more grounded in her own self would help shut out the noise around her.

Unfortunately, self-confidence-building seemed to Cass to be more the purview of a counselor or therapist, which Cass was most definitely not. Not that Lily seemed to mind all that much that Cass wasn't doing much in the *teaching* department. For the most part, more than the lessons, Lily seemed like she just wanted company. She chatted with Cass (and Green, whom Cass found herself unable to shake; if anything, the fae seemed emboldened to appear more often now) about any little thing that came into her mind. Though she'd seemed quiet as a mouse when Cass had first seen her, once she opened up, it was hard to get her to stop talking. On the days when Cass worked—she was scheduled four days a week, usually Monday through Thursday or Tuesday through Friday—Lily spent her free time at the library as well, helping Darcy with projects or reading a book or, after school started, working on her homework.

The school year began the first week of September, after Labor Day. With Lily back at school, Cass's mornings—the few weekdays she wasn't at the library, anyway—were free. She spent that time working on getting the house cleaned out. She'd decided to hold off on the books for the time being and focus on the more straightforward task of culling Aunt Alexandra's clothing. She got most of it boxed up to take to the Goodwill drop-off truck, but a few items were too sentimental for Cass to part with just yet. She knew she'd have to at some point—she couldn't very well hang on to all this junk, what with how frequently she tended to move, and the small apartments she usually wound up renting—but it was still too hard right now. She had plenty of time. She was satisfied with her job at the Riddle Library; Darcy was probably her favorite coworker ever, and Randy was pretty laid-back, as bosses went. Her paycheck was enough to cover groceries and utilities, and since the house was paid off, she didn't have to worry about mortgage payments. There was no rush to get the house cleaned out overnight. She could handle the cleaning day by day.

Besides, it was good for Lily to have a place to go. Cass had soon realized that Darcy hadn't been exaggerating when she'd said Lily didn't get much attention at home. That much became clear the first day school was in session, when she'd come into the library after school, waiting for Cass to get off work at 4:00.

"If you're not taking the bus," Cass had said, removing a book from the shelving cart and replacing it on the shelf, "how do you get home, anyway? Your house is a ways out of town."

"Sometimes I walk," Lily had replied.

Cass's eyes had practically bugged out of her head. "Lily, that's not safe!" she'd cried. It wasn't just the typical stranger danger: the road into the hills where their houses were situated was steep and narrow, with a lot of blind curves that a car might tear around without realizing a pedestrian was nearby. It was also a thickly wooded area that Cass would imagine was prime mountain lion terrain.

"It's all right. My friends watch out for me."

"You can't trust *them* to look out for you," Cass had hissed. When Lily had rolled her eyes, Cass had gone on, firmly, "I'm not kidding, Lily. They might play with you, but they don't have loyalty the way humans do. They don't understand right and wrong the way humans do. They keep you around because you're entertaining to them, but if they decide that they're bored with you—or if they decide that you're so entertaining that they want to *keep* you—you could wind up in some kind of vale that you can't get out of. Forever."

Lily had sighed. "Mr. Green isn't that way."

"Green is *different* and you know it. Don't you pay any attention to what I say to you during lessons? Or what *he* says, for that matter?" She had to give the creature credit—he'd been just as clear as Cass on the dangers of letting your guard down when fae were around.

When Lily shrugged again, Cass had said, "I'm driving you home from now on, okay? Do *not* walk back to your house alone again. Even if I'm not here, you call my cell phone."

Later, Cass had brought it up with Darcy—the part where Lily said she walked home, not the bit about the faery dangers—and to her horror, Darcy had confirmed her story.

"The times I've seen her walking, I've stopped her and driven her home," Darcy had said. "But I know there have been plenty of times I didn't see her."

"Don't her parents care at all? How can they let their nine-year-old daughter walk home by herself when they live so far out of town?"

"I don't think it's that they don't *care*," Darcy had replied, looking uncomfortable. "They just don't seem to *think*. She's supposed to take the bus home; I know that much from one of the times I spoke to them after driving her myself. The problem is that they're never around, so they can't keep tabs on what she's doing. Mr. Kowalski is always at his investment company, and Mrs. Kowalski, she's..." She'd leaned forward, lowering her voice. "She's a lot younger than him. Like, close to our age. I don't think she was ready for motherhood when it happened. She, uh... she spends a lot of time over at the Seven Feathers resort."

The thought of that conversation still made Cass grind her teeth. As if the mother's age was any kind of excuse. If they knew she was walking home when she wasn't supposed to, they should have taken steps to ensure that she stopped. The Kowalskis weren't paying attention to her, and Lily knew it. No wonder she had gravitated to Aunt Alexandra.

But Lily's home life wasn't the only thing Cass had on her mind these days. She kept having the dream. Not the first part, which had seemed, to Cass's relief, to be a one-off. But the last part. She'd be having a normal dream, like the recurring one she always seemed to have about I-5 turning into a roller coaster and her brakes being out, and then all of a sudden, *bam*: We interrupt your regularly scheduled nightmare for one about a thousand times worse.

"We'll all die." Always *"we'll all die."*

The frequency with which this dream was occurring had Cass more than slightly concerned. Recurring dreams didn't always mean premonitions—after all, she was pretty certain that, no matter how often she had that dream, I-5 was not going to suddenly morph into a roller coaster anytime soon.

But Cass had the unshakable feeling that this dream *did* mean something. She just didn't know what.

In the dream, Green and Lily warned her not to disturb the warren. But what was a warren? When Cass had done an internet search for the word, after filtering out people named Warren, she'd found that it was what you called an enclosure for raising rabbits. But she was pretty sure there weren't any rabbit warrens on Aunt

Alexandra's property. That would be a difficult thing to miss.

It seemed logical that the first step to figuring out how to *not* disturb the warren would be to find out what the warren was in the first place. But the question was *how*. Without Aunt Alexandra here to consult, she'd have to figure it out on her own.

Which was how she found herself poking around the non-fiction section of the library that Wednesday afternoon. It was a lull period, with few patrons in the building. Darcy was setting up the children's corner for the first homework hour of the school year, Lily helping her by sharpening pencils. Cass decided to take advantage of their distraction and surreptitiously look for books on local history.

Or at least she *thought* she was being surreptitious. Right up until a male voice behind her said, "So, the librarian is a history lover. Good to know."

Cass nearly jumped out of her skin, whirling around to see Matthew McCarthy standing in the row behind her. The shelves in this section were only half-height, so he could see easily over the top of them. He grinned at her, one hand on the strap of his messenger bag in a casual pose that still somehow made him look like a Greek god.

"So, what's your favorite period?" Matthew asked.

Cass blinked repeatedly at him. "Huh?"

Matthew laughed. "Your favorite historical period," he clarified, gesturing to the shelves before her.

"Oh. *Oh*," Cass said, flushing. "Sorry. Um, I'm not—that is—well, I do like ancient history. Greece, Rome, uh... all of that." She wanted nothing more than for the floor to open up right now and swallow her. She sounded like a complete idiot, even though Matthew was smiling and nodding amicably. "But that's not what I was looking for," she added. "I was looking for some books on local history. Um, you know. Being new in town and... stuff."

"Oh, I saw something a couple weeks ago you may like," Matthew said, moving down the aisle and coming around into hers. "Down here... yeah, here we go. They have some of those Images of America books Arcadia Publishing does." He gestured to a selection of narrow volumes grouped together: *Roseburg*, *Myrtle Creek*, and *Land of Umpqua*.

"That's perfect, thank you," Cass said. Her face was still burning. "Some librarian I am, huh? If the patrons have to show me where books in my own library are."

Matthew laughed. "No worries. You've been here even less time than I have. I won't judge you until you've been here at least another month." He gave her a sly wink that left her rooted in place in a melting puddle, and headed back to the children's corner.

"Hi, Mr. McCarthy," Lily said when she saw him. "Are you helping with homework hour?"

"Every other Wednesday," Matthew said cheerfully. "Are you the only one here?"

"So far," Lily replied, smiling shyly.

"Don't worry, it'll pick up as we get further into the school year," Darcy said.

As Darcy got Matthew situated, explaining the process and getting him signed in to clock his hours, Cass's weakened knees finally gave out and she sank down onto the floor, leaning back against the bookshelf and closing her eyes. She took a few deep breaths, trying to calm her embarrassment—and her pounding heart.

"What are you doing?" she heard Darcy ask a few moments later. She opened her eyes and peeked up to see her coworker standing over her, struggling to suppress her laughter. "You look like you've been struck by lightning. Or were you just struck by the new fourth grade teacher?"

"Will you shut up?" Cass hissed, leaning forward and peering down the aisle to make sure Matthew wasn't looking in their direction.

Darcy chuckled and sat down on the floor beside Cass. "I wouldn't blame you. He is pretty hot. Smoking, in fact."

Cass felt her face burning like a bonfire. "I hadn't noticed."

"Oh, really," Darcy teased. "So you're just sitting here on the floor because it's a comfortable place to be?"

Cass cursed internally. She knew her red face was completely giving her away, but she still stubbornly said, "Seriously, I'm not interested in Matthew McCarthy."

"All right, then, so you won't mind if I make a move on him?

After all, it's not often that an eligible bachelor under the age of fifty shows up in Riddle."

Cass couldn't respond.

It didn't matter, though, because Darcy just laughed even harder. "Okay, okay. I'll keep him out of bounds until after Christmas. But if you haven't made a move by then, I'm not making any promises."

If I'm even still here by Christmas, Cass thought distantly. She was being ridiculous. She had no intention of staying here in Riddle. And she had no intention of dating Matthew McCarthy. She should be telling Darcy, "Sure, go for it!" She should be giving them her blessing. But she couldn't get her stupid mouth to move.

"What were you looking for, anyway?" Darcy asked, changing the subject.

Cass let out a breath of relief, grateful to steer her thoughts in another direction. "Local history. I'm trying to find out more about my aunt's property."

"Oh, there's nothing about that in these books," Darcy said, crossing her legs. "Stuff like that would be in the historical society's files."

"Do you know where their building is so I can check it out?" Cass asked.

Darcy laughed. "Right now it's in my basement. My dad's an officer," she explained. "He's working on organizing the archives to eventually be housed in the Douglas County Historical Museum in Roseburg, but I don't think he's going to be done with it anytime soon. If you want, I could ask him if he's come across anything relevant."

"That would be a huge help," Cass said gratefully.

"Sure thing. I'll let you know if I find anything." Darcy got to her feet, leaning down and offering her a hand. Cass accepted it and stood shakily. "In the meantime, could you do me a favor and clean up the bulletin board in the foyer? It's out of control. If you could recycle anything irrelevant or out of date, that would be great."

Cass nodded and headed into the foyer. Darcy wasn't kidding—it was an absolute mess. Fliers were stacked on top of each other four layers deep. Several of the bill posters hadn't brought thumbtacks, instead attaching their fliers to other papers with tape, which made separating them a tedious matter. By the time she'd gotten the board cleaned off and re-hung the fliers that were still relevant, an hour had passed.

She was just pushing a thumbtack into the corner of a flier advertising the upcoming Fall Fest when she heard a male voice behind her for the second time that afternoon.

"Fall Fest, huh?" Matthew asked.

"Yeah," Cass said, flushing. "Buried under four dozen advertisements for a babysitter, most of them from the same person." Matthew laughed, and Cass asked, "You heading out?"

"Yup. That hour flew by, huh? Lily did her homework silent as a stone, didn't seem to need any help. I sat there reading and feeling useless. But, hey, I get paid for it, so…" Matthew shrugged.

"It will get better as the school year goes on," Cass said with an encouraging smile. "After all, fourth grade is when they learn fractions, right? You'll have the whole class in here by the end of the month."

"Geez, I hope not. That would be one extreme to the other," Matthew said, laughing again. Then he gestured to the notice on the bulletin board behind her. "So, Fall Fest. You going?"

Cass's mouth flapped open and closed a few times soundlessly. "I hadn't given it any thought," she managed at last. "I mean, I just found out about it when I unearthed the flier."

"When is it, next weekend?"

Cass glanced at the flier for confirmation. "Looks like it."

"We should go together. The newbies should stick with each other at times like this."

Cass's mind whirled, looking for an excuse to tell him no—this would be a bad idea—she definitely should *not* go to the Fall Fest with Matthew McCarthy—but to her consternation, her mouth moved of its own accord. "Sure," she said.

"Great," Matthew replied with a grin. "It's in the city park. Do you want to meet here first?"

"Sounds good," Cass replied numbly.

"Great. I'll see you then."

He gave Cass a little wave and, adjusting his messenger bag, headed out the door of the library. Cass stared after him, dumbstruck. She wasn't sure how exactly that had happened, but there was no getting out of it now. She'd made a date with Matthew McCarthy.

Not a date, she reminded herself. *He never called it a date.* But it was as good as one. She needed to watch her step. She'd promised herself after the last time that she *would not* get involved with anyone romantically again. The way her heart was hammering right now spelled nothing but trouble. Whether it happened next week or five years from now, she would eventually get a premonition about Matthew. And there was only one way it could go. The same way it always went for her and her stupid Faery Curse. She wouldn't let her powers destroy yet another relationship.

She had to keep her feelings for Matthew firmly in the Just Friends territory. And then she needed to get out of Riddle. The sooner, the better.

Chapter 9

Over the next week, the town erupted in a flurry of activity. A few days after that Wednesday in the library, Cass noticed a nylon banner stretching over Main Street announcing the upcoming festival. All the local businesses hung signs in their front windows advertising the event and the special deals or menus they'd have available on the big day, or, if they were going to have a booth in the park, an invitation to stop by and see them there. In addition to the typical carnival-style games that usually went along with a festival like this, there was also going to be an Autumn Market where local vendors would be selling everything from vintage clothing to hand-carved wooden curios to flower crowns and bottles of essential oils. There was also going to be a live band and a biergarten. The Fall Fest was big business, Darcy assured her, and she could expect all of Riddle and much of the population of neighboring towns to show up as well.

Cass realized Darcy hadn't been exaggerating as she drove down Main Street the day of the festival. Every parking space up and down the street was full, as were all the parking lots. She wound up parking several blocks away, barely managing to wedge her sedan between a large pickup and an SUV and quadruple-checking to ensure that there wasn't a fire hydrant or an obstructed driveway that could lead to a ticket.

As she walked toward the library, the crowd of people grew thicker. This many people wouldn't fit in the park itself; the street around the park, including around the library, police station, and community center had been blocked off, and pedestrians milled across it, checking out vendor stalls set up on the sidewalk and in the parking lot.

Despite the crowd, Matthew was nowhere to be seen. *He probably couldn't find a place to park, either*, she thought, sitting down on a bench outside the locked library doors. She looked around at what she could see of the park between the crowds. The creek wasn't visible from here today; only the tops of the trees could be seen over the heads of the passersby. The leaves on most of the trees were still completely green, with only a little bit of color showing at the very tops of some of the maples. Autumn was officially starting on Monday, but today it still felt like summer.

A little while later she heard a voice calling her name, but it wasn't Matthew. She looked up to see Lily skipping over to her, her father trailing a short distance behind her.

"Hey, Lily. Are you here with your parents?" Cass asked, glancing at Mr. Kowalski.

"Just my dad," Lily replied, an odd look on her face. Not so much of disappointment—more of resignation. "My mom had plans with her friends in Roseburg today."

"And I'm afraid I won't be here long myself," Kowalski added. "Last minute business meeting, you know how it is." Before giving Cass a chance to respond, he said, "Speaking of which, have you given my offer any further consideration, Ms. Russo?"

"I'm, uh, still thinking about it," Cass said, glancing around to see if anyone was paying attention to what they were talking about.

"Well, the offer still stands, but it won't be open forever. I'm going to need a decision from you soon," Kowalski said, his smile not reaching his eyes.

"Right. I understand. I'm still getting everything sorted, but I'll keep you posted," Cass said, trying to ignore the way her skin crawled when she spoke to him. A premonition, or just dislike for the man?

"Of course," he replied. "Well, Lily, I think we better get going."

"Already?" Lily cried. "But we just got here!"

"I know, but I don't have a choice. I have to get to my meeting, so I need to get you back to the house."

Lily looked crestfallen. Cass hesitated a moment before sighing and saying, "I'll watch her. And I'll bring her home this evening."

"Oh, would you?" Kowalski said, the tone in his voice leading Cass to wonder if he'd been expecting her to make the offer all along. He seemed bored and relieved to have someone taking Lily off his hands. Cass gritted her teeth. "That'd be great. I'll see you both later, then! Be good, Lily," he added in a more stern voice. Lily nodded and sank down onto the bench beside Cass as her father strolled away.

"You're not going to sell Ms. Alexandra's house to him, are you?" Lily asked when he had disappeared into the crowd.

Cass looked at her in surprise. "To your dad?" When Lily nodded, she said, "I haven't decided yet."

"You know what he's going to do with the woods, don't you?" Lily's frown cut deep lines into her cheeks, making her look far older than she was. An adult expression on a child's face.

"I have a bit of an idea, yeah."

Lily whirled on her. "You can't let him! What would happen to my friends if the woods were cut down? They'd have nowhere to live!"

Cass shifted uncomfortably. "They'd find somewhere to move to," she lied.

"No, they wouldn't! They'd just fade away without those trees. You *know* that. You can't do that to them, Ms. Cass!"

If it wasn't before, Cass's skin was *really* crawling now. The words from her dream, spoken in Lily's voice, kept echoing through her mind. *"The warren must not be disturbed. We'll all die."*

Before she could respond, she heard Matthew's cheerful voice call out, "Cass! Lily!"

Lily shot one last glare at Cass before looking up at her teacher. "Hi, Mr. McCarthy," she said, smiling cheerfully as if the conversation of just moments before hadn't even happened.

"Your parents aren't here?" he asked Lily, glancing around.

"My dad just left," Lily replied.

"I told him I'd bring Lily home after the festival," said Cass.

"Do you have any friends you're going to meet here, Lily?" Matthew asked.

Lily's face colored in the bright sunlight. "No," she said, looking down at her feet.

"Well, that's okay. We can keep you company, right, Cass?" He shot Cass a glance, his eyes seeming to ask whether she was okay with this.

Cass felt her heart melt even more than it had at just the sight of him. She'd had no intention of letting Lily wander the festival alone, but she hadn't known how to ask Matthew, for fear that he'd be annoyed by one of his students following him around on his day off. But he'd been the one to suggest it, without a moment's hesitation.

Watch yourself, Cass, her brain snapped, even though the rest of her was resolutely paying zero heed to the voice of reason.

"Absolutely," Cass replied, smiling wide in spite of herself. "What do you want to do first, Lily?"

Lily jumped to her feet. "I want to check out the games at the carnival!" she said eagerly.

The crowd was thick as the three of them made their way across the park. Darcy hadn't been kidding with her estimation that the whole town would be there. The carnival area was set up across the park from the library. In between was the farm produce display area, where farmers across Douglas County had set up booths showcasing their wares and selling the best produce of the season. Cass noticed her neighbor Connie and her husband rooting through the apple selection in the shade of a canvas awning at the Cindersap Orchard booth. Over the last several weeks she'd managed to avoid Connie with the exception of bumping into her once while checking her mailbox, which was mounted next to Connie's on the east side of the street. She hoped her nosy neighbor wouldn't turn now and see her with Matthew. That would be sure to get Connie talking—and talking, and talking...

A small pen housing a nub-eared Lamancha goat stood in the midst of the farm displays, and children crowded around looking at the animal. It stared back at them mildly, the bright sun overhead turning its pupils into rectangular slits. Beside her, Cass heard a small child ask, "What happened to its ears? Did someone cut them off?" and their parent reply, "No, silly, Lamancha goats are born that way!"

The goat wandered over to the fence where Cass and Matthew stood with Lily. As Lily reached out gingerly to stroke the animal,

Cass caught a flash of color on the animal's back. A fae was sitting astride the goat like a cowboy on a fantastically large horse.

And not just any fae.

Lily caught sight of him at the same time and began to suck in a delighted breath, but Cass elbowed her before she could let out the squeal that was clearly on her lips. Lily glanced up at Cass for just an instant before attempting to school her expression—not very successfully, Cass thought with a roll of her eyes. For all of the "lessons" she'd been giving her, Lily still had a long way to go.

"You like goats?" Matthew asked, misattributing Lily's excitement as being directed toward the animal she was petting.

"I do," Lily said, still grinning. "They're so cute! I love their eyes. They look like friendly aliens."

To Cass's relief, Matthew kept the conversation going as the three of them headed to the carnival, which kept Lily's focus on him and away from the fae. How Green had managed to make it all the way from the woods to here, clear in the middle of town a good two miles away—and *why* he'd want to, for that matter—was beyond Cass, but she couldn't very well ask him in the middle of all these people. She looked conspicuously away from the creature, keeping her gaze riveted on the various booths they passed—the dart balloons and the basketball toss and the strength tester—even as he grinned and hopped along after them, weaving in between the people in the crowd. Sometimes he'd brush against an ankle or scurry up someone's pant leg to perch momentarily on their shoulder, and the human would scratch an invisible itch or wave away a fly that wasn't there. No one, of course, appeared to be able to see him apart from Lily and Cass. She wondered if there was no one else in this whole crowd with the Sight, or if any other person who could *see* was, like her, pretending *not* to so as not to draw attention to themselves. A few months ago, that thought would have been laughable to her, but now that she'd met Lily, she was starting to question everything. Growing up, she'd always sort of believed that maybe she and Aunt Alexandra were the only people in the world with the Sight. Now she knew otherwise.

"Do you know what you want to play first?" Matthew asked Lily.

Lily bit her lip, considering. "I want to try to catch a goldfish," she said at last.

Matthew smiled encouragingly at her. "That's always fun. I caught a goldfish at the county fair one time. His name was Trigger. He lived to be almost ten years old." Lily grinned and Matthew added, "But I think we ought to save that one for last. If you catch a fish, they'll put him in a plastic bag of water, and the fish don't like that. You'll want to bring him home right away so you can get him into something bigger. And you'll need food for him, and a nice big tank so he can grow. One with a filter to keep his water clean. That's the best way to give him a long, happy life."

Lily nodded, her expression serious, as if she were mentally filing away all the information he'd just given her.

"Do you think your parents will get you those things?" Cass asked dubiously.

Lily shrugged. "I'll get it one way or another."

Cass quirked an eyebrow at that. "You won't walk into town by yourself, right? If you need someone to take you to the pet store, you come find me," she said. Lily nodded.

"Your parents won't mind you bringing a pet home?" Matthew asked.

"They don't care what I do as long as I don't bother them with it," Lily replied matter-of-factly.

She turned to peruse the carnival once more, looking for a new activity now that the goldfish booth had been tabled for the time being. Over her head, Matthew caught Cass's eye.

"Wow," he mouthed.

"Tell me about it," she murmured back.

Soon the three of them were standing in line for the plastic boat races. Lily eagerly watched as the children ahead of them took their places at the end of a row of modified rain gutters, filled with water. They'd use squirt guns to propel their boats forward down the gutters, the first to reach the finish line winning a small toy prize. A glimmer of color to her left caught Cass's eye, and once again she noticed Green, this time sitting on one of the low branches of a maple tree. Cass sighed.

"Excuse me," she said to Matthew, pulling her cell phone out of her pocket. "I need to make a call."

She left Matthew and Lily standing in line and moved over to the tree, holding her cell phone up to her ear so no one would find it odd if they noticed her talking to herself. "What are you doing here?" she whispered to the fae, who was fanning himself with a five-lobed leaf.

"It's warm today," Green said. "Summer lasts longer now than it used to."

Cass rolled her eyes. "I asked you a question. What are you doing here?"

"Lily was so excited about the Fall Fest, I just had to see it for myself. And I couldn't resist seeing the human you're so tied up in knots over."

"Excuse me?" Cass squeaked. "I don't know what you're talking about."

"Please. Your thoughts have been a tangle for the last week."

Cass gawked at the fae. So he could read her thoughts. She'd suspected as much from the way he tended to answer questions that she hadn't asked aloud, but she hadn't been sure. Since other fae didn't speak English, she didn't know much about them. Could all of them do this? Or, like in so many other ways, was Green different?

"None of the others care enough to try," Green replied, tossing the maple leaf aside.

"Will you stop doing that?" Cass hissed. "It's rude to pry into people's thoughts."

Green snorted. "Manners. A human invention."

Cass gritted her teeth and turned to lean against the tree trunk, not looking at the fae. "How did you get down here, anyway? We're quite a ways from the woods."

"That is a mystery. You don't think I tagged along on that metal deathtrap of yours, do you?" said Green.

"I wouldn't put anything past you at this point," Cass grumbled. Most fae avoided cars because of the iron in them, but she'd already established that Green wasn't like most fae. Besides, just how much iron did modern cars have in them, anyway? Probably not nearly as much as they used to. Maybe not enough to matter anymore. "Just don't make trouble, okay? You've heard the lessons I've been giving Lily. The only way she's going to make it in the human world is if she doesn't let people know she can see you. The last thing we need is you turning up everywhere she goes and distracting her. She wants to be normal."

"Does she? Or is that just what *you* want for her?"

Cass whirled on the creature in exasperation. "Are you kidding me? She's basically a social pariah because of her 'imaginary friends.' No kid wants to be seen as a freak."

"Maybe she just hasn't met the right humans yet. Like your human who's always yelling at you on your talky box." He gestured to Cass's cell phone. "She believes you. She would love to be able to see us."

"Emma is different, okay? Emma is..." Well, to be honest,

Emma was a bit of a freak herself. That was why she and Cass had gotten along so well when they met. But there was no guaranteeing that Lily would meet someone like Emma.

"Listen," Cass snapped, leveling a glare on the fae. "I'm just trying to protect her. This world is full of people who aren't content to live and let live. If they encounter someone who seems to see things that aren't there, or hear voices that no one else can hear—they're going to be treated like they're crazy. Do you want to see Lily locked up in some mental hospital because her parents or one of her teachers think she's got something wrong with her?"

Green swung a spindly leg back and forth from the branch on which he perched. "Do you think your Matthew would do that?"

"He's not *my* anything!" Cass hissed, lowering her voice. "And honestly... I don't know. I don't know him, okay? He seems nice, but that doesn't mean he believes in... the supernatural, or whatever."

The fae grinned, his pointy features seeming to grow even sharper with the expression. He suddenly looked quite devious. "Have you tried asking him?"

"What? No—look, stop trying to change the subject. The point is, I know what I'm talking about here. I'm just trying to keep Lily safe. So do *not* interfere, you got that?" She jabbed her index finger into the fae's tiny sternum.

The fae grumbled, rubbing his chest. "Fine. Have it your way."

Cass nodded and started to turn, putting her phone back into her jeans pocket. She barely heard Green mutter, "You didn't use to be so distrusting."

Cass glanced at him over her shoulder. "Excuse me?"

"Nothing," Green replied innocently, climbing higher up into the maple tree and out of her line of sight.

"Everything all right?" Matthew asked when Cass returned to the booth. A colorfully-painted sign above it read *Rain Gutter Regatta*. Lily was next in line, hopping eagerly in place as she awaited her turn. "You seemed a little... agitated on the phone there."

"It's nothing. I'm fine," Cass replied, forcing a smile.

"Okay, good," Matthew said, smiling back.

The game operator gestured for Lily and a redheaded girl behind her in line to come forward. The girls eagerly hurried to their respective gutters and the operator handed each of them a plastic squirt gun to control their boats with. Matthew moved to the sidelines, pulling out his phone to record the race.

The bell dinged and the girls began squirting their water pistols. The crowd around them shouted out encouragement, but Cass barely registered it. Green's question was still in the forefront of her mind. *"Have you tried asking him?"*

She hadn't. And she wouldn't. That was something you just didn't chance, no matter how much you thought you trusted the person. Meeting Emma had been pure good luck, but she knew better now than to count on lightning striking twice. After all, Emma had already *believed*, even if she couldn't *see*. But trying to get someone who *doesn't* believe to accept that there could be more to the world than they know? Even someone who said they loved you could turn around and call you crazy.

She'd learned that lesson the hard way. It was a risk she wouldn't take again.

Chapter 10

Lily wanted to play almost every carnival game, and she had the tokens to do it. With the money her father had given her—stowed neatly in a coin purse hanging around her neck—she'd bought enough tokens, Cass was certain, to make the Fest organizers weep with joy.

By late afternoon, Cass was fairly exhausted. She'd forgotten how much energy a kid at a carnival could have. When Matthew had asked her to come with him to the Fall Fest, she'd envisioned a leisurely afternoon sitting in the biergarten, listening to local musicians and enjoying a craft beer or maybe some fresh apple cider. But she supposed she should have known better. Lily had been just about glued to her side every day for the last three weeks—why should today be any different?

Miraculously, the three of them managed to find an empty picnic table to sit at around four o'clock, when Matthew suggested they grab an early dinner from one of the food trucks to beat the later crowds. They'd gotten food from the Asian fusion booth, and, after stacking her massive stash of carnival tokens into two neat towers before her, Lily dug into her plate of stir-fried noodles eagerly.

Cass watched her, barely feeling energetic enough to half-heartedly stir a fork through her fried rice.

"You hanging in there?" Matthew asked, looking at her with an amused quirk of his eyebrow.

"Barely," Cass admitted. "How many kids do you have in your class this year?"

"Around thirty," he said.

Cass grimaced. "I don't know how you do it."

"Years of practice," said Matthew. "Beginning with babysitting my two younger sisters from the age of thirteen on."

"Ah. That explains a lot. I'm definitely lacking in experience there," Cass said.

"Do you have any siblings?" Matthew asked.

She shook her head. "Only child." She wondered if her life would have been different if she'd had a sibling. Would he or she have had the Sight as well? Would she have had someone to share her troubles with? Or would they have disbelieved her as much as her parents had?

"Me too," Lily said, quickly swallowing a mouthful of noodles. She flashed Cass a grin, a smear of soy sauce leaving a dark mark beneath her lower lip. "Two lonely only children."

Involuntarily, Cass found herself smiling back at the girl. "When do you ever have a chance to get lonely?" she asked, handing her a napkin and gesturing to her chin. "You spend every waking moment hanging around my house."

"I'm just keeping you company," Lily said cheerfully, wiping her face and then taking another bite of stir-fry.

"Excuse me," a small voice said then. Cass glanced up to see a redheaded girl who looked to be about Lily's age. She looked vaguely familiar, and after a moment Cass remembered her as the girl who'd been behind them in line for the plastic boat race.

"Do you want to play horseshoes?" the girl asked Lily, her face red with embarrassment. "None of my sisters or brothers want to, and you have a lot of tokens..."

Cass glanced past the girl to see a gaggle of younger children, most of them also redheaded, accompanied by parents who looked frustratingly less exhausted from dealing with five kids than Cass did from dealing with one. *Years of practice,* Matthew's voice echoed in her head.

"Sure!" Lily said eagerly, scooping up the token pile and jumping to her feet.

"Whoa, whoa, hang on a second," Cass said, jumping to her feet as well. She smiled awkwardly at the girl before pulling Lily aside and crouching down to her level. "Do you know this girl?" she whispered.

"We raced boats earlier," Lily replied. "She's nice. When she was standing by me during the race, I heard some of her thoughts," she admitted, sounding chagrined. "Even though she has brothers and sisters, she doesn't have a lot of friends. She's homeschooled, so most of my classmates don't talk to her. She's lonely, too."

Cass squeezed her eyes shut. This was exactly what she was worried about. "Okay, remember what I told you before? Just because you can read some of a person's thoughts doesn't mean you know them. Also, you're supposed to be trying *not* to read people's thoughts, right?"

Lily let out a breath of annoyance and looked away. "I *am* trying," she muttered.

Cass's frown softened. "I know you are," she said more gently. "You just need to be careful, okay? I know you saw Green here earlier. I don't know where he went, but if you see him, you can't talk to him in front of..." She glanced at the redheaded girl.

"Amelia," Lily said.

"Right. Amelia. You can't let her know about your... your *friends*."

"Okay, okay."

"I mean it, Lily!" Cass hissed.

"I understand!" Lily snapped back.

"Everything okay?" Matthew interrupted, coming over to the two of them.

Cass jerked upright. "Everything's fine," she said quickly. "I was just warning Lily... you know, stranger danger."

Matthew laughed. "You're really not used to small towns, are you? Don't worry. Amelia's family goes to my church. Lily will be fine with them."

Cass sighed. "All right. But don't leave the park, okay?" she said to Lily. "And come find me when it starts to get dark. I told your dad I'd bring you home, remember?"

Lily nodded eagerly and raced over to where Amelia was waiting with her family. Cass watched them, silently praying that Lily really *had* been paying attention during their lessons.

"You and Lily seem close," Matthew commented.

Cass shrugged. "She lives next door to me. And you know how her parents are. She's starving for attention."

"Yeah, I've noticed," Matthew said. "But I think it will be good for her to have friends her own age. And the Reynoldses seem to be a good family, but I'm sure Amelia would like to have other friends besides just the kids she sees at church youth group."

"You're right," Cass admitted. If Amelia and Lily could become friends, it would be good for Lily—especially once Cass left Riddle. It would probably be fine as long as Lily kept her mouth shut about her Sight. The damage had been done with her classmates, but Amelia didn't seem to know about those rumors. It could be a clean slate if Lily played it smart. "I guess I just don't want her to get hurt."

Matthew laughed. "You sound like a parent. Kids have a way of getting under your skin, don't they?" Before Cass could come up with a retort to that, he said, "And now we've got the rest of the day to ourselves. I was thinking biergarten, how about you?"

Cass stood frozen in place, working her jaw soundlessly for a moment, her mind an absolute tangle between *You sound like a parent* and *We've got the rest of the day to ourselves.* Matthew seemed to have a singular talent for turning Cass into a tongue-tied mess.

Finally she just sighed and gave him a smile. "That sounds perfect," she said.

Cass followed Matthew over to the large pole tent, nestled among some trees near the creek. She could hear the sound of music coming from inside, drowning out the sounds of the carnival as they drew closer. A portable picket fence was set up around the pole tent, allowing for outdoor seating in the pleasant evening breeze beside the running water. As they passed one of the picnic tables inside the fence on their way to the entrance, Cass heard a cheery voice call out her name. She turned her head and saw Darcy waving at her. She sat at a table with an older man and woman that Cass assumed must be her parents. Her father had snowy white hair, but her mother's hair was dark like Darcy's, with just a few threads of silver running through it. Her mother sat in a black self-propelled wheelchair with bright blue trim, a matching blue floral backpack hanging from its handles.

She and Matthew waved back at her before entering the pole tent. Strings of lights crisscrossing over their heads gave the tent a cheery golden glow, enhanced by the setting sun streaming in through the cut-out windows in the canvas walls. Tall black speakers amplified the sounds of the band playing across from the entrance, a hipster folk trio playing a fiddle, a small bongo drum set, and a mandolin.

"Kind of loud in here," Matthew commented, leaning toward Cass and raising his voice.

"Do you want to sit on the patio?" Cass yelled back.

Matthew nodded. "I'll get us drinks. Do you have a preference?"

"Cider is good if they have it. I'll find us a table."

Cass pushed through one of the side flaps out to the fenced-off area where they'd seen Darcy. The patio area was so full that Cass thought they might be out of luck, but then she noticed an upturned barrel with a square piece of plywood set across it, just large enough for two people to sit. She hurried over, sitting on one of the stools and setting her purse on the one beside it to claim the seats.

A moment later she was joined at the table by Darcy, her gap-toothed grin wide. "Hey," she said, shoving Cass's purse across the plywood tabletop and perching on the edge of Matthew's stool. "How's the date going?"

Cass rolled her eyes. "It's not a date."

"Mm-hmm. Sure."

"Seriously," Cass said in a low voice. "We've been babysitting Lily Kowalski for most of the day."

"Are you kidding me?" Darcy replied, her voice rising in a disbelieving squeak.

"Nope. You didn't expect her parents to actually spend a day with her, did you?"

Darcy sighed. "I suppose not. So where is she now?"

"She went off with another little girl and her family," Cass said, hoping the worry she still felt wasn't overly apparent in her voice or on her face. "Amelia Reynolds."

"Oh, they live on my street!" Darcy said cheerfully. "They're nice. I wish I could get them to come to events at the library more. Community outreach is a you-know-what." She shook her head, then gave Cass a sly grin. "So, you're technically not Lily-sitting anymore. There's still time to turn this non-date around, you know." When Cass squirmed uncomfortably, Darcy laughed. "Fine, fine, I'll lay off. I wanted to tell you—my dad and I found some stuff about your aunt's property."

Cass sat up straight, her eyes widening. "Really?"

"Yup. We still have a couple boxes to go through to make sure there's nothing else, and then I'll bring it all to you at work next week. Are you scheduled on Monday?"

"No, I'm off on Monday," said Cass.

"It'll have to be Wednesday, then—I'm off on Tuesday." She

leaned forward, lowering her voice, and added, "I don't know what you were looking for, but there's some crazy stuff in some of those articles. Your aunt's property has quite the storied history."

Goosebumps rippled across Cass's arms. *You don't know the half of it,* she thought.

"Hey, Darcy," Matthew said just then, approaching the table with two mason jars full of amber liquid. "How's it going?"

"Good, good. I won't keep you two, I just had a work question for Cass," Darcy said quickly.

"Are you sure you don't want to join us?" He looked around for another stool, but there were none to be had.

"Seriously, I'm sure. We're going to be heading out soon," Darcy replied, gesturing to where her parents were still sitting with her thumb. "Have a good night, you two!" She gave them a little wave and squeezed away between the tables.

When she was gone, Matthew turned back to Cass and gave her a conspiratorial grin. "Is it rude that I'm sort of relieved?" he whispered, sliding Cass's cider over to her across the plywood tabletop. "I mean, Darcy is nice. I just was hoping we could finally get some one-on-one time, you know what I mean?"

Cass couldn't respond. Those words made her heart leap clear into her throat, cutting off access to her vocal cords. *Stop it, Cass,* her mind warned. *Seriously, stop it—*

Her face burning, she took a long sip of her cider and chose to ignore her inner voice of reason for the evening. The cider tasted good, sweet without being *too* sweet.

"So, how are you settling in so far? Are you liking Riddle?" Matthew asked, and Cass felt herself relax at the change of subject.

"It's definitely different than I expected," she said, choosing her words carefully. "I guess I'm not used to small-town living."

Matthew laughed. "You kind of give off that vibe. Where did you live before?"

"Most recently San Jose, in California. But I've lived all over the place. Mostly the West Coast since college, but before that my family lived in Chicago."

"You move a lot?"

"Yeah," Cass admitted. "I can never seem to stay in one place for more than a year or so. Aunt Alexandra used to say I had itchy feet."

Matthew laughed. "So, what about Riddle? You think you'll stay here awhile? Or are your feet already getting itchy?"

"It's hard to say," Cass said noncommittally. "But how about you? You haven't been here that long yourself. How are you liking Riddle?"

"It's a nice little town," Matthew said. "I mean, I've only been here two months, so things could change. But I have a good feeling about it so far. I'm definitely a small-town guy, though. The town I grew up in wasn't that much bigger than Riddle. I think the biggest city I've lived in is Eugene, and that's not exactly a metropolis."

"Have you always lived in Oregon?" Cass asked.

"I'm technically from Washington, but Foreston—the town where my family lives—is just over the Columbia River, so not that far off."

"Foreston," Cass repeated. "That name sounds familiar."

"It was one of the towns affected by the fire in the Gorge a couple years ago," Matthew said.

"That's right. I heard about it on the news. Was your family okay?"

Matthew nodded. "Luckily, the fire only brushed the outskirts of our town. We were worried about my parents' house for a while there, but it turned out okay. The hollow tree protected us," he said with a laugh.

"The hollow tree?" asked Cass.

Matthew colored and shook his head. "It's nothing. Just a dumb superstition in my town." He hesitated, as if weighing whether to say more; but just then, movement out of the corner of her eye caught Cass's attention, and she looked away from Matthew. In the low branches extending over the patio, Cass noticed a couple fae scurrying. Wood sprites by the look of it. They had long, narrow heads the gray-brown color of bark, with soft mottling around the cheeks and noses. Cass would have looked away, except she noticed a third fae with them—Green.

What is he up to now?

"Um—so, how's Tucker taking the move?" she stammered, trying to keep her distraction from showing. She'd just given Lily a lecture on not reacting to Green, and here she was doing the same thing. She knew better than this.

"I think he likes it better here," Matthew said. "We lived in an apartment in Eugene, so he didn't have a yard. I'd have to walk him in the morning, then run home while the kids were at lunch to let him out, and then walk him a couple more times in the afternoon and evening. That got old real quick, I'm telling you. But I was able to rent a house here, so he at least has a yard to run around in and burn off his energy." He rolled his eyes and added, "Hopefully he doesn't drive the neighbors *too* insane when he runs around in circles barking at the sky."

Cass laughed, imagining the giant Doberman galloping around Matthew's backyard, his ears flopping about him, trying not to trip over his own paws.

Her laughter was interrupted by an acorn dropping down from the tree directly onto Matthew's head—with a bit more force than that of gravity alone.

Matthew flinched, blinking as the acorn bounced down onto the table in front of him, then looked up at the tree. "What the heck?" he said.

Cass followed his gaze and saw Green sitting between the two wood sprites as they laughed, a noise like the squeaking vocalization of a Western gray squirrel. Cass narrowed her eyes at him, and the fae gave her a sly, angular grin.

"Squirrel fight?" Cass suggested weakly, looking back at

Matthew.

He snorted. "I can see that. *That's my acorn!*" he mimicked in a high squeaky voice. "*'Nuh-uh! It's mine! Take that!'* And then he throws it at him, misses, and the rest is history."

Cass couldn't help but laugh at that. "Now it's no one's acorn, little morons," she said once she caught her breath.

Matthew shrugged. "Squirrels are definitely not known for their deductive reasoning skills."

As he spoke, a small clump of dried oak leaves dropped down on him. This didn't have the force of the acorns, but Cass recognized the origin all the same. They fanned out as they fell, some landing on Matthew's shoulders and in his hair, and a particularly large leaf dropping neatly into his mason jar of beer.

"Oh, my gosh," Cass hissed in exasperation.

Matthew laughed, brushing the leaves off himself. "Man, those squirrels really have it in for me," he said. He looked up at the tree and called, "I'm didn't mean it! Squirrels are the smartest! You've got more gray cells than Hercule Poirot!"

"Little brats ruined your drink," Cass muttered, picking the leaf out of the amber liquid and pointedly not looking up even as she heard Green's tinny hoots of laughter above her head.

"It's fine. It wasn't all that great to begin with," Matthew admitted.

"Maybe we should sit somewhere else," Cass suggested. "We could go inside. The squirrels can't bother us there."

"Unless they chew a hole through the roof of the tent and drop down on us like little squirrel cat burglars," Matthew said.

Cass shook her head. "Please do not even say that in jest," she replied, and Matthew chuckled.

"Wouldn't put it past them?"

"Definitely not." Especially not these "squirrels." She shot one last glare at Green and picked up her cider, following Matthew back inside the pole tent.

The hipster folk trio had changed their instruments, swapping the mandolin for a banjo and the bongo drums for a wooden kitchen chair which the drummer rhythmically hit with drumsticks along the top rail and in between the decorative wooden spokes that made up the chair back.

"They have an interesting repertoire," Cass commented as she and Matthew sat at an empty table. Inside the tent, actual tables had been set up in lieu of the upturned barrels, and small votive candles burned inside mason jars.

"They do, but it has a cool sound," Matthew replied.

The music from the band was too loud to allow for conversation, but it felt comfortable, somehow, just sitting quietly together and watching the trio perform, the banjo player at one point setting down his instrument and grabbing an extra pair of drumsticks, he and the drummer banging out an intense rhythm on the wooden chair while the fiddler moved her bow across the strings at a frantic pace. Cass got so wrapped up in their performance that for two whole minutes, she almost forgot about Green altogether.

She didn't even notice the mason jar with the candle inside sliding closer to Matthew's hand, resting in a gentle curl on the tabletop, until the hot glass connected with his skin. He let out a curse along with a hiss of pain, recoiling away from the candle.

"Are you okay?" Cass asked, her eyes widening as she saw the flash of green disappear over the side of the table.

"I'm fine, I'm fine," Matthew said, shaking his head dismissively. "I didn't even see that thing. It's my fault. Geez, I'm so clumsy tonight."

"It's not your fault," Cass said, glaring at the fae as he skittered between the feet of a middle-aged man walking by and disappeared out one of the tent's side flaps. "Do you need ice?"

"No, no," Matthew said quickly. "I'm fine."

"Well, put your hand on this at least," she said, sliding her half-empty cider over to him. It wasn't as cool as it had been, but it was better than nothing. "And if you'll excuse me, I'll be right back."

With purpose, she marched out the flap that Green had disappeared through. This door led back out into the main fair rather than the patio area. The sun had dipped low enough on the horizon to cast the park in semi-darkness, but it still only took a moment to locate the fae, sitting in the branches of a nearby tree.

She barely paid any mind to the crowd of passersby other than giving a cursory glance to make sure no one was paying attention to her. Then she stormed over to the tree and put her hands on her hips. "What is wrong with you? Why are you picking on Matthew so much?" she demanded.

Green spread his long-fingered hands and gave her an innocent look. "I was just trying to get a reaction," he said.

"Well, you got one. Are you happy now?"

Green smiled deviously. "You're not the one I was trying to get the reaction out of."

"What are you talking about?" Cass asked.

But Green didn't get a chance to answer. Behind Cass, Matthew cleared his throat.

Cass whirled around, wild-eyed. "Matthew," she stammered, "look, I know this probably looks crazy, me standing here yelling at a tree. But I can explain..." *How* she was going to explain, she had no idea, but she had to come up with something, fast.

"Wait," Matthew said, holding a hand up. *Too late.* She braced herself for what was inevitably coming next: *"You don't need to explain, but actually, I think I need to get going,"* followed by weeks of awkward avoidance until she finally left town. If she was lucky, he might not tell the rest of the town she was insane, at least not until she was gone. Maybe it was for the best. After all, she was clearly getting in way over her head here. Matthew deciding to break it off now would probably be the best outcome for everyone. Then she could leave Riddle behind with no regrets.

If only the thought of that didn't sting so much.

"Before you say anything else, can I ask you a question?" Matthew said, an odd tone in his voice, suddenly serious and almost shy. "I know this is going to sound crazy, and I understand if you never want to talk to me again after this and write me off as a total lunatic. But I have to know."

Cass stared at him, her head quirked in confusion. This conversation wasn't going in the direction she'd expected. "What is it?"

"You..." He hesitated, then blurted it out. "You don't happen to see faeries, do you?"

Chapter 11

"Are you freaking kidding me?" Emma shrieked. "The grocery store guy knows about the fae?"

Cass hadn't been able to wait until the morning. It hadn't mattered that it was after midnight on the east coast by the time Cass got home from the Fall Fest. She'd needed to talk to her best friend *immediately*. Still in a state of shock, she'd shoved the door open and sat right down on the foot of the stairs to call Emma. It was impossible. Matthew knew about the fae. Matthew *believed* in fae.

When he'd asked her that question outside the biergarten, she hadn't been able to respond. She just stood there, silently opening and closing her mouth over and over, her mind such a whirl of confusion and disbelief that she was pretty sure that her brain had shut off everything except basic motor function. Finally, distantly, she processed the sound of Green in the tree behind her shrieking and whooping with laughter. No wonder the little monster had been following her all day, goading Matthew like that. He knew.

He had to have known.

"Have you tried asking him?"

"Hang on," Cass had finally managed to stammer out. "Are you telling me... are you saying you believe in fae?"

"Never mind," Matthew said quickly, starting to turn away. "I'm sorry, never mind. I can't believe I said that—"

"Wait!" Cass cried, rushing over and grabbing his hand to keep him from leaving. Matthew froze, glancing down at their clasped hands in surprise. Cass quickly let go, her face burning. "Don't go," she said softly. "I just... no one ever believes."

They stood a moment in silence, Matthew's eyebrows raised halfway up his forehead. "So... it's true? You can see them?"

"I can," Cass whispered. "Can you?"

"I can't, but my sisters can," Matthew replied.

Cass blinked at him in surprise. "Seriously?"

"Yup."

She blinked again. "You can't see them yourself, but you believed when your sisters said that they're real?"

He gave her an odd look. "Of course I did. Why shouldn't I? They're my sisters."

Cass had suddenly found that tears were biting behind her eyes. He'd believed his sisters that fae existed, even though he couldn't see them himself. He believed Cass. Cass's own parents had never believed that the fae were anything but her own imaginary game, something that was cute when she was a child but worrisome as she got older. She'd had to learn to hide, to keep secrets from her own parents, to keep them from trying to send her to a psychologist. Only Aunt Alexandra's intervention on her behalf—and her warning to Cass to be more careful with whom she shared her secret—had kept them from thinking she was insane.

And though she'd been so guarded with her secret ever since, five years ago, it had almost happened again. She told the truth, and someone who said he loved her—who said he *trusted* her—looked her in the eyes and told her she was crazy.

But Matthew... Matthew believed what his own eyes couldn't see. As if there was nothing to it. As if it was no big deal. *Because they're his sisters.*

"All right, it's official," Emma blurted over the phone. "If you don't marry him, I want him."

Cass shook her head, clearing away the mist of her reverie. "That's not funny, Emma."

"What's the matter with you? He's hot, he's obviously interested in you, and he knows about the fae. You couldn't ask for someone more perfect!"

"You know I can't get serious about him," Cass said. "Or anyone. It's too dangerous. You remember what happened last time." It wasn't just about being able to see fae. If that's all it was, there would be no problem. It was what went *with* that. Emma of all people should have known that. She should have remembered.

"Cass, what happened to Jeremy wasn't your fault."

"He sure blamed me for it," Cass replied darkly.

Emma's voice rose in protest. "Yeah, but Matthew is

different—"

"I'm not going through this again, Emma!" Cass snapped. "I already made a promise to myself. I swore up and down that I was not going to get serious about another guy. I'm not going through that again."

The line was quiet so long that Cass almost wondered if Emma had hung up on her. Then Em said, softly, "All you're doing is punishing yourself. Do you think you deserve that? And do you seriously think Jeremy was worth doing this to yourself?"

Cass sighed and squeezed her eyes shut. "This isn't about Jeremy, okay?"

"It sure as heck sounds like it is."

"Look, forget it. Just forget it, okay? I'm not staying in Riddle, Oregon for the rest of my life. I'm not getting tied down just because some schoolteacher happens to believe in faeries. I know who I am. I'm not going to let myself forget it."

"I think you're making a mistake, Cass," Emma said quietly. "But it's your mistake to make. Good night."

And with a soft click, the phone went silent. Cass lowered it from her ear and looked up at the pendant lamp over her head, the way the colors from the Tiffany shade bounced off the ceiling. The house was quiet. Even Onyx hadn't made an appearance since she'd come in the front door. She was all alone.

She slumped over sideways on the staircase and cried until there was nothing left to cry.

Chapter 12

"Oh good, you're here," Darcy said as Cass came through the door of the library on Wednesday morning. This was possibly the first time Darcy had made it to work before her since Cass had started her job at the library. The truth was, Cass had seriously considered calling out today. It wasn't just that she was completely fatigued from the combination of the last month's events and weeks of sleeping poorly (especially over the last three days). It was also that today was Matthew's scheduled day for homework hour, and she wasn't sure she could face him again.

But even as her finger had hovered over Randy's phone number to call in sick, she hadn't been able to go through with it. There was something more important she needed to do today, and that was to—hopefully—finally get some answers about what this recurring dream meant. She'd had it again, every night since Saturday, and every time, to her utter humiliation, it included the first part of the dream that had come with it all those weeks ago, before she'd even known Matthew's name. If anything, it was even worse now, because now she *did* know him. And as time passed, it was getting harder to convince herself that this wasn't a future she wanted, that she didn't secretly hope that this dream was a premonition and not just a fantasy of her own making. Every day while she was awake, she found herself thinking about him, wanting to know more about his sisters and the fae of Foreston. He'd only texted her once after the Fall Fest, to say he'd had a good time and that he hoped they could do it again sometime soon. He probably didn't want to be pushy, but Cass had found her emotions careening wildly between relief that he hadn't texted again and longing that he would, reaching for her phone to text him herself only to delete the text and push the phone away. Her mind knew that she couldn't do this, that she had to keep Matthew firmly in the friend zone. If only she could get her heart to cooperate.

Regardless, she needed answers. She had to find out what the warren was. And her best bet was the documents that Darcy and her father had dug up. If nothing else, Cass needed to get those at least. If worse came to worst, she could always feign a headache and use it as an excuse to go home early, before Matthew showed up for homework hour.

"Sorry," Cass said, removing her jacket and stowing it and her purse in the cubby behind the front desk. "I had trouble getting going this morning."

"I've got you covered," Darcy said, sliding a cup marked with the Pony Espresso logo across the countertop to her.

Cass breathed out a grateful sigh. "You're the best."

"I figured you'd need it when you read this," Darcy said, holding up a manila folder full of papers.

"Is that the stuff about my aunt's property?" Cass asked, surprised at how thick the folder was.

"Yup. And I'll tell you what, you're in for a treat," said Darcy. "Growing up we always used to say the Russo house was haunted, but once I got to be an adult, I figured that's just what any kid would say about a big old Victorian house, you know what I mean? But after reading that, I can see how the rumors got their start. The original owners of the house were a little... how should I put this... eccentric?"

"Oh?" Cass said, flipping open the folder and lifting the first stapled packet of papers from the stack.

"Yeah. Mrs. Porter was widowed young, and she got big into the nineteenth-century spiritualist fad. She had all sorts of weird ideas about her property. It kind of reminded me of—what's it called? You know, you lived in San Jose."

"The Winchester Mystery House?" Cass supplied, only half paying attention as she flipped through the papers. The first two packets were photocopies of newspaper articles from around the 1940s; the rest of the folder was filled with handwritten pages, yellowed and faded. They appeared to be notes from an in-person interview with Hannah Porter, the original owner of Aunt

Alexandra's house. The handwriting looked familiar to Cass, but she couldn't quite place it.

"Yeah, that one. Only instead of thinking that she needed to keep building her house until she died, Mrs. Porter's beliefs were more about the woods the house was built in."

Cass's head jerked up. "Seriously? What did she think about the woods?"

"Do you know anything about Victorian spiritualism?" Darcy asked.

"Not much," Cass admitted.

"Basically there's a lot of references to a veil that separates this world from a spiritual world. Mrs. Porter seemed to think that the woods were kind of... right in the middle of that veil, if that makes sense. Almost like the woods *were* the veil, maybe," Darcy said. "She called her property 'The Wood Between the Worlds.' And she believed that there was a direct portal to the other world somewhere in the woods. She believed it was her job to protect that portal. She called herself the Chatelaine. Essentially she saw herself as the caretaker of the woods. She believed she had to safeguard the woods, or else the veil would break down and the world would be overrun with evil spirits."

Cass felt her skin ripple with gooseflesh. This was it, she knew it. The portal that her house's original owner was talking about—that had to be the mysterious warren. "Did she say anything about faeries or anything like that?" She regretted the words as soon as she asked them, but they seemed to burst out of her mouth unbidden.

Darcy gave her an odd look, and Cass's face flushed. "Yeah, she did. How did you know?" Darcy asked.

Cass shrugged, quickly glancing back down at the papers to avoid looking Darcy in the eye. "My aunt used to tell me that story. That there were faeries in the woods. I wondered if she might have heard it from someone who knew Mrs. Porter."

"Your aunt knew Mrs. Porter, actually," Darcy said.

Cass looked up in surprise. "What?"

"Yeah, look at the last page of that interview."

Cass flipped to the back of the packet. It was signed *Alexandra Russo, 1953*. That would have been when Aunt Alexandra was twenty-eight, two years younger than Cass was now. This interview with Mrs. Porter had been conducted by Alexandra herself.

"From what I gathered, your aunt befriended Mrs. Porter when she was a child. She mentions that they encountered each other at the 1939 World's Fair in New York and kept in touch."

Another chill ran over Cass's skin. Aunt Alexandra would have been thirteen or fourteen at that Fair. Cass didn't know how they met, but she had a suspicion she knew how they'd befriended one another. If Mrs. Porter had the Sight—and it sure as heck sounded like she had—then it almost certainly had something to do with that. Had Mrs. Porter seen Alexandra reacting to something that anyone else might think wasn't there? Or had it been the other way around? Either way, they must have connected over their shared Sight, and kept in touch for that reason, most likely through letters until Aunt Alexandra was old enough to travel to Riddle on her own. Had Mrs. Porter been a guide to Aunt Alexandra the way Alexandra had been to Cass, and then to Lily?

"All I know is that when Mrs. Porter died in 1955, she left her house and all her possessions to Alexandra," Darcy said. "That's the last thing in the folder, a copy of Mrs. Porter's will."

Cass's breath caught in her throat. She'd never thought about how her great-aunt had acquired her house—she'd just always had it. She'd had it for decades before Cass's own birth, and it had never occurred to Cass to ask the story behind it. That was just the way it had always been. *She was the same age as you when Mrs. Porter left her the house,* she realized.

And now Cass knew the reason why Aunt Alexandra had never moved away from Riddle, had never followed through with her dream of retiring to Greece or some other sunny clime. Mrs. Porter had believed she was meant to be the caretaker of the house and the woods, and had clearly left the position of Chatelaine to Aunt Alexandra. And Alexandra had taken it seriously enough to forgo her own dreams and stay here. But had her great-aunt actually expected Cass to take up the same mantle when she left the house to Cass in her own will? She knew that Cass wanted to have nothing to do with the fae. And she'd never mentioned a word of this to Cass in advance. Never given her a hint of the responsibility she planned to lay on her grandniece's shoulders.

Probably because she knew I'd never go for it if she had told me, Cass thought. For the first time, she felt annoyed with her great-aunt. She'd loved her grandpa's sister more than her own grandmother, but the woman had been keeping secrets from Cass her whole life. The more time she spent in Riddle, the more things she learned that Alexandra had been hiding from her. Now what was Cass supposed to do?

"Thanks, Darcy," Cass finally said. "Wow. This is a lot to unpack."

"Yeah, pretty crazy, huh?" Darcy replied with a laugh. This information clearly hadn't affected her the way it affected Cass. Well, why should it? To anyone else, it would just sound like a kooky legend, something local kids would whisper about and rational adults would shrug off as some eccentric woman's delusion from some bygone century. They couldn't know how real it was to someone like Cass.

"Yeah, crazy," Cass agreed with a shaky laugh, putting the papers back in the manila folder and shoving it into the cubby with her jacket and purse.

By afternoon, Cass had made a decision. As much as her rational mind had been urging her to avoid Matthew, after thumbing through the papers Darcy had given her more thoroughly during her lunch break, she realized that she wouldn't be able to untangle this riddle on her own. If she wanted to find out what the warren was—and what her premonitory dream was trying to warn her about—she needed help from an expert. And with two sisters with the Sight, Matthew was the closest thing to an expert Cass had.

She was going to have to ask for his help.

She was in the stacks shelving books when Matthew came in for homework hour that afternoon. He gave her a little wave as he passed that made Cass's stomach flip-flop, then went to join Lily at the table in the kid's corner. No kids besides Lily had shown up at all so far this school year, but Darcy was still nonplussed. She was convinced they'd start pouring in around report card time, in early November.

Cass waited to approach the table until Darcy had left for her fifteen-minute break. There were no other patrons in the library; just Lily quietly working on solving math problems out of a worn textbook, and Matthew reading another mass market paperback— it looked like Ursula K. Le Guin today—and waiting for Lily to ask him a question or for some other kid to come in.

Now or never, Cass thought as she approached the table with the papers Darcy had given her.

"Hey," she said, holding the manila folder awkwardly behind her back.

Matthew looked up from his book. "Oh, good," he said with a grin. "I was worried you were avoiding me. I didn't want to push you or anything... I mean, I know I dropped a bombshell on you on

Saturday."

Cass felt her face grow red. She tried not to dwell on the fact that, were it not for these papers Darcy had given her, she *would* be avoiding him. "Yeah, no. It's fine," she said. "I just... needed some time to process it."

"I can imagine. I could tell it was a surprise. Do you not know many other people"—he paused, glancing at Lily, who was diligently working on her math homework and pointedly pretending to ignore their conversation—"uh, you know."

"I didn't until recently." Cass sighed and said to Lily, "I know you're listening. Yes, we're talking about your friends."

"Really?" Lily eagerly shoved the binder paper and pencil away from herself and leaned against her elbows. "Does Mr. McCarthy see them, too? I thought I... uh, heard some stuff."

Cass rolled her eyes and gave Lily a glare. "I thought we were going to be working on *not* listening in."

"I *am*!" Lily protested. "It's hard!"

"Wait," Matthew said, looking back and forth between the two of them. "Lily has the Sight as well?"

"Yup. This town seems to be just crawling with people who do."

Matthew *hmm*-ed. "That's interesting," he said thoughtfully. Then, to Lily, he explained, "I can't see them. But I know about them from my family. My sisters can see them."

"Cool!" Lily replied eagerly. "There are more people like us than we thought."

"You still have to be careful," Cass admonished.

"I *know*," Lily grumbled.

"Anyway," Cass said, turning back to Matthew. "I had a question for you. Have you ever heard of a thing called a warren?"

"I have!" Lily interrupted.

Cass looked at her in surprise. "You have?"

Lily nodded. "Yes. Mr. Green said I have to stay away from it."

Cass arched an eyebrow. "Well, that's..." *Ominous*. Her mind automatically went back to the warning dream, which Lily and Green were both a part of. "So, what is it?"

"I don't know. He just told me to stay away from it."

"Very helpful, Lily."

Matthew laughed. "I do know what a warren is, yes." When Cass whirled on him in surprise, he clarified, "Well, I don't know specifically what the definition is. But I know that there's one in Foreston."

Cass blinked, her mouth partially open. "Seriously?"

"Yeah. It's a hollow tree that grows on the Paine Estate. That's a big Victorian house museum in town. My sisters say that the fae seem to hang out there. Sort of like... they come from there, maybe."

Cass's skin prickled. *She believed that there was a direct portal to the other world somewhere in the woods.* That's what Darcy had said about Mrs. Porter. Could it be...?

"Like a door, maybe?" Cass suggested.

Matthew considered. "Yeah, maybe. You're thinking a door to wherever it is they come from?"

"Right. A door to the other world."

Matthew nodded. "Could be."

Cass inhaled. This was it, she could feel it. This had to be the warren that the dream was talking about. Mrs. Porter's hole in the veil. "So you're saying it's a tree?"

"The one in Foreston is. I don't know if they're all the same." He looked at Cass as she gnawed on her lip. "What's this about?"

She sat down at the table across from Matthew, Lily between them on the table's end. She slid the manila folder across the table to him. In confusion, he opened the folder and started pulling papers out.

"I... I think there's a warren on my aunt's property," she said, unsure of how to explain. She didn't know whether Matthew knew or believed in so-called faery blessings—just because his sisters had the Sight didn't mean they had any abilities beyond that. And she didn't want to go into full details about her dream in front of Lily. There was always the chance Lily may have already heard her thoughts about the dream, but if she hadn't, Cass didn't want to alarm her.

"There is," Lily said, leaning forward in her chair to try to look at the papers Matthew was riffling through now. "Remember? Mr. Green told me to stay away from it."

"Why is that?" Cass asked, trying to sound casual. "Did he say it was dangerous?"

"He said it could be for me."

Cass narrowed her eyebrows, but before she could say anything, Matthew spoke.

"Look at this, Cass," he said, sliding the paper across the table and pointing to a line of Alexandra's faded handwriting. Cass read the words, *"The Wood Between the Worlds."*

"Darcy said that Mrs. Porter called the woods on her property that," Cass said.

"That's from the Chronicles of Narnia," Matthew said.

Cass's eyebrow rose, and her stomach churned slightly at the memory of the book she'd seen in his back pocket that day, the same book he was reading in her dream. "Oh?" she managed to say, swallowing.

"Yeah. In *The Magician's Nephew.* The sixth book written but chronologically the first. The wood is filled with ponds, and each of the ponds is a portal to another world," Matthew explained.

"Like the warren?" Lily asked.

"Could be," Cass said. "When was that book published?"

"Sometime in the 1950s. 1955, maybe?" Matthew answered.

Cass's skin tingled. "That's the year Mrs. Porter died."

Matthew let out a long exhalation. "Now that's what I call a creepy coincidence."

Cass frowned. She'd long ago lost her ability to believe in coincidences. But by the same token, she seriously doubted that

Mrs. Porter and C.S. Lewis had been acquainted. *Unless* they *somehow ran into each other at the 1939 World's Fair*, she thought wryly.

"Maybe there's more than one wood like this one," Lily suggested. "Mr. McCarthy said there's one in Washington, too, right? Maybe there was one where Mr. Lewis lived, too."

"He may have at least heard legends about it, even if he never encountered it himself," Cass said, nodding slowly.

"Actually"—Matthew pulled his phone out of his pocket as he spoke, tapping a quick search into the browser—"now that you mention it, I remember reading a while ago that Lewis was inspired by another fantasy author. Here it is. William Morris. He wrote a book called *The Wood Beyond the Worlds* in 1894. I bet if we did some more digging, we'd find that the name's been passed down through folklore a lot longer than that, even. People have been seeing fae for thousands of years. They had to have known about these special woods, too."

"And it all boils down to the same thing—the portal, or the warren, whatever it is," Cass said. "The opening in the veil. That must be what makes the woods... the way they are." Dripping with fae and other magical nuisances. She remembered the way she'd been pixy-led her first night in Riddle and shuddered. Powerful enough to overwhelm even a seasoned pro like Cass.

"Are you guys talking about Mrs. Porter?" a voice over Cass's shoulder asked. Cass jumped and turned. Darcy had returned from her break and was standing right behind her. She'd been so wrapped up in Matthew's theory, she hadn't even noticed.

"Um, no," Cass said quickly.

"Wait," Darcy said, looking from Cass to Matthew to Lily. "Are you saying it's true?"

"I didn't say that—"

"It's true," Lily said eagerly.

Cass whirled on the girl. "Lily!" she hissed.

"It's fine! You can trust Ms. Hudson," Lily whispered back, tapping the side of her head.

Cass squeezed her eyes shut in frustration. Did Lily not listen to a word she said?

But it was too late. Darcy had pulled out the chair beside Cass and sunk into it. "Wow. I knew there was something weird about that place! So all that stuff about the woods and the veil, it's really real?"

Cass hesitated. How would Darcy react to this? Would she be like Emma, or... Jeremy? Every fiber of her being resisted just blurting this out, but Lily had left her boxed in a corner, and now she couldn't see a way out of it. She was just going to have to take the plunge.

"It's real," she said, trying not to wince as the words left her mouth.

Darcy's grin grew wide, revealing the gap between her front teeth. "Oh, my gosh! Seriously? That's amazing! So, can you guys all see the faeries? Is it cool? Or is it scary? Oh, Cass, does that mean your house really is haunted?"

Cass paused a moment before answering, her brain frantically trying to keep up. Darcy didn't think she was crazy. It made Cass shaky with relief, though she knew it would take a while for her mind to process that she now had two friends—and she realized then that, yes, she did consider Darcy her friend, not just her coworker—who believed her about her Sight.

Well, two friends and Matthew. Whatever Matthew was. A friend, right? Yes, a friend. *Keep him in that friend zone, Cass.*

"I'm not sure," she answered finally. "I can't see... you know, ghosts. Or spirits, or whatever. Only fae."

"Ah, okay," Darcy said. "Do you think maybe some people can see one but not the other? That would explain why there are so many ghost hunter shows but not as many faery hunter shows."

"Probably," Cass said numbly.

"But Mrs. Porter seemed to see both. Do you think maybe she had extra powers? Is that a thing that happens? Having more than one power?"

Cass squeezed her eyes shut. Oh, yes. It definitely *was* a thing.

"That seems logical," Matthew agreed. "Just from skimming this interview, it does seem that her Sight was genuine. I don't see any reason to doubt it."

Great. A fae infestation *and* a haunted house, and Cass could only verify one of them. Just what she needed.

"Listen, the ghost thing isn't important right now," she interrupted. "What matters is this warren. If there is one on my property, I want to know where it is."

Darcy let out a small gasp. "That's right! You own the house now, and you can see the faeries. That must mean you're the new Chatelaine!"

Cass felt her teeth grinding of their own accord. That was the last connection she wanted Darcy to make. It just reinforced the obligation that Aunt Alexandra had left her without her consent.

"What's a chatelaine?" Lily asked curiously.

"It's like a caretaker," Matthew explained. "The Paine family were the original caretakers of the Foreston warren. When the Estate became a museum, the museum docents sort of took it on. They watch over the warren and keep it safe."

"Right," Cass said, pouncing on the opportunity to turn the conversation back in the direction of the warren. "And if I'm supposed to keep it safe, I need to know what it is and where it is. Lily, did Green tell you where the warren is?"

Lily shook her head.

"Well, how are you supposed to stay away from it if you don't know what or where it is?"

"He said I'd know it if I saw it. And if I saw it, I should go away from it."

Cass squeezed her eyes closed in exasperation. Of course he had. And of course he wouldn't give Cass a straight answer about it if she asked, either. He found Cass's troubles far too amusing to offer help, and he seemed incapable of being direct in any conversation. What was the use of a fae who spoke English, anyway? He was barely better than the rest of them. Just more of an annoyance.

"If you need help searching your property, maybe I could help," Matthew suggested. "I don't have the Sight, but I've seen the one in Foreston. Maybe I would recognize your warren if I saw it. We could look this weekend. I'm free all day Saturday."

Cass hesitated, but she couldn't help but see the logic in his suggestion. Still, all day alone in the woods with Matthew...

Friend zone, Cass, friend zone!

She turned to Darcy. "What about you? Do you want to come along?" she asked. But she knew it was a no-go the second her eyes met Darcy's and she saw her friend's sly expression.

"Sorry, Cass, I can't make it. I have to take my mom to a doctor's appointment in Roseburg."

A doctor's appointment on Saturday? Cass was so sure. But she could tell by the grin on Darcy's face that no matter what day she suggested, Darcy's curiosity about the fae would be outweighed by her meddlesome need to try to push Cass and Matthew together.

"Can I come?" Lily asked.

"Absolutely not," Cass said. "Do you not remember what Green said to you?"

"But why do you get to go, then?" Lily asked, her mouth

turning down in a pout.

"Because we're grown-ups. I have more control over my abilities, and Matthew's been around warrens before."

Lily folded her arms and slumped down in her chair. Cass leaned over and nudged her. "Besides, I thought you were going to Wildlife Safari with Amelia on Saturday," Cass reminded her.

That made Lily brighten a bit. The girl hadn't been able to shut up about how much fun she'd had with Amelia after the fair. And Cass's day off on Monday had been uncharacteristically quiet, since Amelia and her mom had accompanied Lily after school to the pet store in Myrtle Creek to get a tank and supplies for her new goldfish. Cass was still a little nervous, especially considering Lily's overly trusting nature, but Amelia seemed to be a good friend for her to have.

"My property is pretty big," Cass said, turning back to Matthew. "Are you sure you're up for it? It's about a hundred acres of overgrown trails and wooded property."

"Sounds like an adventure," Matthew said cheerfully. "I'll bring lunch. And I'll also bring Tucker. We can tell him he's there to guard us and then make fun of him behind his back when he spends the whole day barking at the sky and cowering at his own shadow."

Cass felt her mouth turn up in spite of herself. "You're so mean to that dog."

Matthew laughed. "You'll see how you feel after a full day of his shenanigans."

Cass snorted and said, "All right. We'll look for the warren on Saturday, then."

"And you'll be sure to text me any important updates," Darcy added, her voice laden with meaning.

"Sure thing," Cass said, resisting the urge to roll her eyes. It didn't matter what Darcy thought was going to happen on Saturday. Matthew would not be leaving the friend zone. They'd find the warren, Cass would hopefully get to the bottom of what her nightmare was trying to warn her about, Matthew and Tucker would go home, and everything would be fine.

Everything would be fine.

Chapter 13

Saturday morning was gray and cold. Cass wrapped herself in a blanket as she went downstairs. Even though it was still stuffy in the upstairs bedroom—especially since Cass refused to open the screenless windows—she'd noticed that it was starting to get chilly in other parts of the house in the early hours of the day, and today was possibly the chilliest yet. She shuffled around the kitchen in her sock feet to assemble her breakfast of Cheerios and coffee. Her stomach was tied in too many knots to get down more than a few bites, though. She told herself she was just nervous about looking for the warren today, but she knew that that was only half of it.

The smaller half, to be honest.

After dumping the soggy bowl of Cheerios into the sink, she checked the weather forecast on her phone. It was supposed to warm up in the afternoon, but stay in the fifties and low sixties for most of the morning. She decided dressing in layers would be best. By nine o'clock, after checking her hair and makeup for the seven hundredth time (even though she told herself after every check that it didn't *matter* how she looked, this was *not* a date, and she should *not* be worrying about whether Matthew found her attractive or not, she was supposed to be keeping him in the friend zone), she decided she'd had enough of sitting inside fidgeting. She'd go sit on the front porch. That way they could jump right into the search as soon as Matthew and Tucker arrived.

There was a wooden bench on the wraparound porch, and Cass sank into it, watching for the sight of Matthew's vehicle on the driveway. The air was brisker than she'd expected, considering how hot it had been last week. She rubbed her hands over her arms in her cardigan, trying not to shiver and wondering if she should go inside and find something heavier to put over the sweater.

Before she could move, though, she heard a high, reedy voice ask, "What are you up to?"

Cass looked up with a start to find Green perched on the porch railing, swinging his little legs back and forth casually. *Now he shows up?* she thought in mild annoyance. She hadn't seen him for a few days; he seemed to disappear periodically, and it was hard to predict his comings and goings. She considered not answering his question, since she was sure he already knew anyway. But there was always the chance that he might decide to be uncharacteristically helpful today. So finally she answered, "Matthew and I are going to look for the warren today."

Green's mouth was pulled up into a crooked smile. "Is that so?"

Cass looked at him in surprise. That wasn't the reaction she'd expected. "Aren't you going to try to talk me out of it?" she asked.

Green considered her for a moment. "Do you want me to?"

Cass sighed. Elusive as always. She didn't know why she'd even entertained the notion that he might for once actually be forthcoming. "You told Lily not to go near it," she pointed out.

"That's true," he agreed. "But that's because I know things you don't know."

Cass wasn't sure if it was his words or the way he said them, but a wave of goosebumps rippled across her skin. *And what exactly* does *he know that he's not letting on?*

Aloud, she merely said, "That sounds a little… sinister."

"It's not meant to sound one way or the other," he replied, his legs still swinging. "It's just true. If you take the truth to be sinister, maybe the problem is on your end."

Cass closed her eyes and took a calming breath. *Keep your temper.* "Well, then," she said, "if you don't think I should stop, why don't you give me directions so I know where to go?"

"I can't do that," Green said.

"Why not?" Cass asked in frustration.

"I just told you," Green replied, seeming affronted.

"Why do you enjoy being so obtuse?" Cass snapped. So much for keeping her temper. "Why don't you ever just answer me straight?"

Green shrugged. "Because I can't."

"*Can't* or *won't?*"

Green didn't respond immediately. He seemed to be thinking this through as if it were a puzzle. "What's the difference?" he asked eventually.

Cass rolled her eyes. He was being deliberately evasive, she was sure of it. She decided to change tack.

"Why is this thing so hard to find, anyway?" she asked. "Matthew made it sound like everyone in town knows where the warren in Foreston is. It's practically a tourist attraction. But I can't find a single hint as to what or where the warren here is."

Green snorted. It sounded like a sneezing chipmunk. "The hollow tree fae have grown too comfortable. The humans have sworn to protect their warren. They're safe, and it's made them lazy." He narrowed his eyes at Cass and added, "But *these* woods are anything but safe."

Cass felt her skin crawling once more. His words were loaded, full of meaning, but she couldn't guess what that meaning was. Not safe for whom? And not safe from what?

"What do you mean by that?" she asked quietly.

Green got to his feet, brushing off his knobbly knees with his spindly hands. "What a stupid question," he said. "You know what I mean."

"No, seriously," Cass said, but her words were interrupted by the far-off sound of a dog barking. She turned her head just in time to see Matthew's silver pickup pulling into her driveway. When she turned back to Green, the fae had disappeared. She let out a groan. As always, her interrogation tactics had left her with nothing. Whatever she and Matthew were going to find today, it looked like they were on their own.

Tucker's barking grew louder until Matthew had parked behind Cass's sedan and shut his truck off. Then, through the glass of the windshield, translucent behind the reflection of pine branches overhead, she saw the dog's silhouette jumping around the cab of the truck, in and out of Matthew's lap as he attached a leash to his collar. Cass couldn't help but smile as the haggard-looking Matthew finally emerged from the truck, Tucker's leash in hand. The Doberman was wearing a doggy coat made of red plaid flannel. Combined with his soft floppy ears and his doofy expression, Cass found herself wondering how anyone could consider a dog like Tucker threatening. Did cropping their ears make them seem more intimidating? Or were they all just big idiots whose owners thought they could trick the world by altering their natural cuddly ears?

"You look worn out already," Cass commented, coming down the front steps to greet Matthew.

"This knucklehead will do that to you," Matthew said, adjusting the straps on the hiking backpack he'd slung over his shoulders. "He usually isn't that bad in the car, actually, but when he sees a pedestrian he tends to go a little bananas. And, unfortunately, your neighbor across the way was doing work in her yard."

Cass tried not to wince. So Connie had seen Matthew arrive, then. It would be all over town by the end of the day.

"Do you want to come inside for some coffee?" Cass offered. She'd finally restocked the pantry with some fresher grounds and the fridge with a variety of flavors of Coffee mate, so now she could actually be a decent hostess. Not that she'd had any visitors besides Lily thus far, but still.

"That would be great," Matthew said.

Cass led Matthew and Tucker up the steps but paused before opening the door. "How is he with cats?" she asked.

"Terrified," Matthew replied.

"It's just that my aunt..." She trailed off. Was Onyx *her* cat now? She supposed he was, for the time being at least. He had started sleeping on her bed after just a couple days of her being there, although he never stayed through the night—he usually got a wild burst of energy around three A.M. and she could sometimes hear him running up and down the stairs yodeling at the ceiling. "That is, I have a cat," she finished.

"He'll be fine," Matthew assured her. "He'll probably fall over in a heap like a fainting goat at the sight of it."

Cass chuckled at that visual and opened the door, leading Matthew through the maze of rooms back to the kitchen. Once there, she gestured for him to sit at the round wooden table in the breakfast nook while she poured coffee into a plain white mug, the only one in Aunt Alexandra's collection that wasn't covered in illustrated flowers, puppies or kittens. He took a little bit of sugar but no cream.

"Thanks," Matthew said when she handed him the mug. "Some warmth for the road. It's chilly out there."

"Fall finally showed up," Cass agreed.

Matthew took a swallow of his coffee. "This house is huge. I can't believe your aunt kept it up all by herself."

"Tell me about it," Cass said. "I've been working on sorting out her estate, but it's overwhelming."

"You probably have some brownies and household elves running around helping you, at least," Matthew said.

Cass felt her cheeks grow hot. "Uh, no," she said. *Not anymore, anyway.*

"Really? That surprises me. My sister Laney volunteers at the Paine Estate, and the fae there always help out with the chores. I guess I figured it would be the same everywhere with a warren. You know, an exchange—the caretaker watches over the woods, and the fae help the caretaker with their home. Or museum, in Laney's case."

"Maybe it's different everywhere," Cass suggested. She didn't want to tell him that she'd chased the brownies out on her first day here. It seemed his sisters had a drastically different philosophy on fae than she did. They seemed to be a lot more at ease with them, based on Matthew's own comfortable acceptance. But his words did have her wondering: if Alexandra had accepted her role as caretaker, is that why she'd let the fae into her house? Sort of a mutual benefit?

But she had to have known Cass would never accept a role like that for herself. Alexandra knew Cass couldn't stand having fae too close to her; it was why she'd given her the tip about the colander. Had she just assumed Cass would outgrow her aversion to the supernatural? That had clearly been a mistake. And where did it leave Cass now?

Cass was pulled from her thoughts by movement in her periphery. She looked up just in time to see Onyx stroll into the kitchen. Tucker, who had been standing next to Matthew with his chin resting on the table, looking mournfully around for a bit of food to snatch, froze. Onyx hesitated in the doorway, the long black fur on his tail silently puffing out. He stared at Tucker, his green eyes wide as saucers. Then, after a moment's consideration, he strutted directly over to the newcomers.

"Be nice, Tuck," Matthew said, holding the dog's collar.

Tucker took a step back, but Matthew's grip on his collar was firm. Completely unconcerned by the size of the canine before him, Onyx wrapped himself around the dog's ankles. As Cass watched, Tucker began to tremble.

Cass giggled in spite of herself. "He really *is* afraid," she whispered.

"I told you," Matthew replied, grinning.

Onyx rubbed himself against the dog's legs a couple more times, then went over to Matthew and wrapped himself around his ankles for good measure.

"Wow, you weren't this lovey-dovey to me the first day I was here," Cass said to the cat. Onyx shot a look at her that seemed to say, *I wasn't sure if you were going to throw me out on my ear the way you had the brownies.* She flushed defensively before realizing how preposterous it was to be reacting to what she *imagined* her cat was thinking.

As she watched him, Onyx turned his nose up and strolled over to his food dish by the sink. He took a few bites of kibble while Tucker cowered. Cass struggled to suppress her giggles once again when Tucker, still cowering, raised his front paw weakly to point at the cat, as if to say, *Excuse me, there is a cat over there.*

After a couple mouthfuls, Onyx decided that he was bored with this interaction and vacated the kitchen once more. Tucker collapsed in a heap the second the cat disappeared.

Cass burst out laughing, and Matthew laughed along with her.

"I told you," Matthew said, trying to catch his breath. "This dog is a marshmallow."

"You weren't kidding! He's, like, ten times Onyx's size and he was scared stiff! Poor Puppy Tucker," Cass cooed, reaching over to stroke the dog's soft ears. "Life is rough, huh?" He looked at her with his sad brown eyes, as if in agreement.

"Well, let's get a move on before the cat comes back and

Tucker goes catatonic," Matthew said, downing the last of his coffee and standing up to set the mug in the sink. "Hopefully we won't find anything too terrifying out there, such as—Heaven forbid—a raccoon. Or, worse, a deer. Tucker is petrified of deer. I think he thinks they're bigger Dobermans, and he's not sure whether they want him to join their pack or kick his butt."

Cass laughed once again. But this time her laughter brought with it a sense of foreboding that she couldn't quite shake. *"Hopefully we won't find anything too terrifying out there."*

"I know things you don't know."

"These woods are anything but safe."

She refused to let her worry show. But she still found herself thinking, *It will be a good day if the worst thing we find out there is a deer.*

Matthew clipped Tucker's leash back onto his collar and slung his hiking backpack over his shoulders once more as Cass opened the kitchen door and gestured him down the side steps into the yard. He looked around the overgrown garden with interest. They stopped at the edge of the yard where the various forest trails forked off.

"Which way should we go?" Matthew asked. Tucker looked back and forth between them, his stub wagging gently beneath his flannel coat.

"I already went down that one. I didn't see anything out of the ordinary," Cass said, gesturing to the path that led to the rose garden and into the woods beyond. She shuddered at the memory of her first night in Riddle. She chose not to mention the faery ring that had bewitched her.

"Okay, so should we just work from left to right?" Matthew suggested, pointing to the leftmost trail. "I'm guessing most of these will wrap around in a circle, so we'll probably come back on one of these other paths."

"Sounds like a plan," Cass agreed.

They made their way down the uneven path into the woods. The trees were beginning to turn in earnest now, reds and oranges and yellows seeping down from the tops of the trees like a bleeding watercolor. The colors stood in bright contrast against the snatches of pale gray sky peeking between the branches overhead.

"So, how are your feet doing?" Matthew asked out of the blue. Cass looked at him in confusion and he laughed. "You know, that whole itchy thing. You sick of Riddle yet?"

Cass considered this. Truth be told, she was actually less sick of this little town than she would have expected. When she'd arrived a few months ago, she'd been eager to get Alexandra's belongings sorted quickly so as not to spend any more time here than was necessary. But it had been a couple weeks now since she'd done any purging in earnest. There was her job at the library, and her lessons with Lily after work and on weekends, and of course trying to solve the mystery of the warren... she didn't have a lot of time. That was what she told herself, anyway; but if she was being honest, she'd have to admit that she didn't feel overly enthused about getting it done quickly. The longer she was here, the harder it was for her to imagine not seeing Darcy every day, or Lily, or...

Other people.

She sighed. "Not *just* yet," she said at last.

"That's good to hear," Matthew replied cheerfully. "It's rough being the new guy in a small town. It's been kind of nice to have someone to go through the growing pains with."

Cass felt her face grow hot, warmth spreading across her cheeks out to her ears. She wasn't sure how to answer, but fortunately Matthew kept talking so she didn't have to.

"You said before that you've moved a lot. Where all have you lived?" he asked.

"All over the place, really. Up until sixth grade my family lived outside Dayton, Ohio. Then we moved to Chicago, and my parents still live there."

"Where'd you go to college?"

"University of Illinois at Chicago for undergrad. Then I got my MLIS at the University of Washington in Seattle," Cass said.

"Is that when your West Coast wandering began?"

"Yeah," Cass replied. "I've lived in San Diego, San Bernardino, Sacramento, San Jose... lots of S cities."

"Geez, you really can't stay in one place, can you?" said Matthew. "What are you, the Littlest Hobo? Is there a voice that keeps on calling you?"

Cass's eyebrows rose. "Excuse me? The what now?"

Matthew grinned. "You don't know the Littlest Hobo? Canada's answer to Lassie?"

Cass laughed aloud. "I missed that one."

"My grandparents live in Saskatchewan," Matthew explained, "so we used to watch it when we'd go visit them in the summer. My sisters and me. Much better show than Lassie. It's got a German Shepherd instead of a Collie. White and black with reverse mask markings. We had a dog like that growing up—he was a Malamute mix—so when my sisters and I were little, we always pretended that the Hobo was Beau. That he kept on wandering until he found our family, and then he decided we were too cool to leave and decided to settle down."

He had a wistful expression on his face as he spoke, and Cass smiled at this glimpse at Matthew's childhood.

"Tell me more about your sisters," she said after a moment. "What are they like?"

"Annoying," Matthew replied bluntly, making Cass laugh again. "No, seriously," he protested. "They're always rubbing it in that they have the Sight and I don't. Even now that we're adults. Do you know what it's like to be bullied by your kid sisters?"

"I wouldn't, being an only child and all," Cass teased. "But I can imagine it probably *would* be annoying."

Tucker stopped to mark a tree they were passing. He'd been doing that every fifty feet or so. "He needs to leave a trail in case we get lost. Then he can lead us home," Matthew explained.

"Ah," said Cass.

After a moment, Matthew said in a more serious tone, "Honestly, my sisters are pretty cool. I think you'd like them. My middle sister, Laney, is about a year and a half younger than me. Her Sight didn't use to be as strong as Taryn's, but it's improved since the fire, bizarrely."

"Wait," Cass said, looking at him in confusion. "What do you mean not as strong?"

"Our grandma used to compare it to regular vision, right? Sometimes you have 20/20 vision, and sometimes you need glasses. Taryn's got 20/20, and you seem to as well. But Laney... Growing up, Laney could *see*, but she said it was blurry. Like walking around without your glasses. Or your contacts, in my case."

"I didn't know that was possible," Cass confessed. "Although I didn't know anyone else with the Sight until I moved here. Apart from my aunt." She'd learned so much since she moved here, more than she ever could have expected. "But her vision changed?"

"Yeah, a few years ago."

"During the forest fire?" Cass paused, remembering their conversation at the Fall Fest. "You said then that the hollow tree protected the town. Do you mean the warren?"

"Yeah," Matthew said. He ran a hand through his honey-brown hair self-consciously. "I felt like a class-A idiot when I blurted that out last week. But I guess that worked out, didn't it?" Cass smiled back at him, and he went on, "Anyway, Laney volunteers at the museum. The Paine Estate, where the hollow tree is. Something happened during the fire. We were getting reports on the news that the flames were getting close to the museum grounds, and Laney went running out there like... well, like the impulsive redhead that she is. Like she was going to fight the fire all by herself. But maybe she did after all. I've never been able to get a straight answer out of her, but Paul said—oh, Paul's her husband—anyway, he said it was like the warren called out to her that night. And after that, her Sight got clearer. Like the fae wanted to reward her or something."

"Wow," Cass said. "Like a faery blessing?"

"Yeah," Matthew said. "So you've heard that term, too? I wasn't sure if it was something our grandma made up."

"My aunt had a book about it," Cass explained. "I found it when I was sorting out her library."

"Do you have one?" Matthew asked.

Cass hesitated. "Have what?"

"You know, a faery blessing."

"I wouldn't exactly call it a *blessing*," Cass admitted.

Matthew let out a laugh that echoed off the trees. Tucker

turned to look at him over his shoulder.

"Can't be that bad, can it?" Matthew asked when the laughter subsided.

Cass shrugged. "It's a bit of a mixed bag."

"Can't be worse than Laney's."

"Oh, yeah?" Cass arched her eyebrow. "What's Laney's, then?"

"She's a seamstress, and her mood affects her sewing. Not like the stitches come out bad if she's cranky or something," he added when Cass gave him a confused look. "More like... one time when I was in high school, I asked her to fix the trousers of my band uniform for me. She was so annoyed with me for asking her to do it that the next time I wore them, I fell down the bleachers and broke my leg."

Cass stopped in her tracks. "*What?*"

Matthew nodded. "Yup. If she sews when she's in a good mood, it will bring whoever wears the clothes or whatever good luck. But if she's in a bad mood... you're better off just chucking whatever it was into the incinerator."

Cass stood there blinking, trying to process what he'd just told her. And then she found herself once again wondering if these talents would be more accurately described as faery *curses*. "Well, what about Taryn?" she said at last.

"Taryn's isn't too bad. She sometimes gets memories from objects she touches. I could see how that could get a little annoying, but it's never seemed to bother her all that much. The fae must have liked her better than Laney when she was born, since her Sight was more clear, too."

Cass wasn't sure if she'd consider that a plus, but Matthew seemed to.

"But you don't have any Sight at all?" she asked him.

He shook his head glumly. "But I think—well, never mind. It's probably silly."

"What?" Cass asked.

He hesitated a moment, looking directly at Cass. His warm brown eyes locked with hers. "I don't have the Sight, but I think I might have a blessing," he said at last.

"Really?" Cass said, trying to ignore the way the intensity of his gaze had melted her insides.

"Yeah. Sometimes I... well, I get these feelings. That I need to go somewhere or do something. Overpowering feelings. Like an instinct of some kind, but stronger. That's why I've always wondered..." He trailed off and then shrugged. "Never mind. It's probably stupid."

Cass took a step closer to him, putting her hand on his shoulder. "It's not stupid," she said firmly. "I... That is, mine is... kind of similar."

He smiled tentatively at her. "Yeah?" he said, but to her relief he didn't push it. He left it to her to decide whether she was going to share her own story with him.

She was tempted, but she found she couldn't quite bring herself to form the words. Not yet.

"Yeah," she said softly.

He held her gaze a moment longer, a gentle smile teasing the corners of his lips. Then the two of them continued down the wooded trail together.

Around noon they stopped in a clearing between the trees to eat lunch. A fallen tree lay on the edge of a small meadow, the tall spring grass turned brown by the summer sun, the dried remnants of wildflowers peeking in clumps between the straw-colored blades. Cass and Matthew found a spot on the fat trunk of the fallen tree where orange mushrooms hadn't yet begun to grow, and the two of them sat, Matthew slinging his backpack onto the ground and unzipping it. He pulled out a large empty Tupperware container, which he filled with cool, clear water from a Thermos. He placed that on the ground for Tucker to drink out of. The clouds had mostly burned off by now, and sun filled the clearing. Cass had stripped off her cardigan and Matthew had pulled off his own jacket as well as Tucker's flannel coat. He pulled two paper sacks out of the backpack, handing one to Cass, and then shoved the sweater and jackets into the leftover space of his backpack.

Cass peeked inside the paper sack and grinned. Matthew had

packed a peanut butter-and-jelly sandwich, along with an apple and a small bag of Kettle chips.

"Nothing wrong with the classics," Matthew said, and Cass laughed.

Tucker loomed over Cass as she ate her sandwich until she gave him her crusts. Then, once he realized there was nothing left for him, he began to snuffle around the log while Matthew pulled his phone out of his pocket and opened up the uView video app.

"I'm surprised you can get a signal out here," Cass said.

"You're not that far out of town," Matthew replied distractedly. Then he turned his phone around for Cass to see. "Here. For your erudition."

Cass took the phone and pressed play on the video. It was the opening credits for *The Littlest Hobo*, the Canadian *Lassie*. Cass laughed as she watched the German Shepherd running across a field with a hunting rifle and flying in a hot air balloon.

"That song is going to be stuck in my head for the rest of the day," she said, handing Matthew his phone back.

"You're welcome," Matthew said cheerfully.

Cass laughed again, taking a bite out of her apple. After she swallowed, she asked, "So you said earlier that your grandma knows about the Sight. Does she have it, too?"

"She did. She passed away a few years back."

"Oh, I'm sorry," Cass said.

"No worries," Matthew replied.

"Was she the one who lived in Saskatchewan?"

Matthew shook his head. "No, that's my grandma on my mom's side. She and my maternal grandpa are both still living. My paternal grandparents lived in Foreston, but they both passed while I was in college. They were quite a bit older than my mom's parents. My dad was a change-of-life baby. It was rough on my sisters especially, though. Grams had always been someone they could turn to for advice about..." He trailed off and looked at her meaningfully.

"I definitely understand that," Cass said softly, reaching for the key around her neck and rubbing it between her fingers.

"You and your aunt seem like you were close. I can see why."

Cass nodded. "Yeah. She taught me so much, but I feel like she left me with more questions than answers. All this about the warren, and being a caretaker... she never told me anything about it. I never knew that she was keeping so many secrets from me."

"Is that out of character for her?" Matthew asked.

"I thought so. But maybe I didn't know her as well as I thought."

"Maybe she had a reason for doing it the way she did," Matthew suggested.

"Maybe."

"Well, at least you're not alone in trying to figure it out."

Cass couldn't meet his eyes. She looked around, trying to keep her gaze focused on anything other than Matthew beside her, just a hand's breadth away. That was when she noticed Tucker, standing stock-still a few feet away from them, staring at the mushrooms at the end of the fallen tree and pointing with his front paw.

A second later, she saw what he was pointing at: in between the natural orange mushrooms sat a mushroom-capped gnome. It was taunting Tucker, making faces and jeering.

Matthew followed Cass's gaze but saw only the dog. "He's doing it again," Matthew said. "Pointing at nothing. Cowering before his own shadow."

"He's not pointing at nothing," Cass said.

"He's not..." Matthew broke off, suddenly realizing what Cass was getting at. "You mean—there's something there?"

"Yup. A gnome."

Matthew's jaw worked soundlessly as he processed this. "You mean Tucker can see fae?"

"Looks like."

Matthew considered for a moment. "Do you think all dogs can see them, or just some?"

"I have no idea. I've never had a dog before," Cass answered.

Matthew sighed. "You know, Laney or Taryn could have told me this before. They've both seen how skittish Tuck is. They probably thought it was funny, the brats."

Cass tried to resist chuckling. "I'm sorry," she said.

Matthew's grim expression began to crack. "Typical, isn't it?"

"I'm beginning to think it is."

They held their serious expressions just a moment longer before bursting into laughter that echoed across the clearing.

By late afternoon, Cass's calves were killing her and she was beginning to doubt that there was such a thing as a warren, at least here in these woods. The trails had turned out to be a veritable maze, with numerous forks and intersections along each one. To keep from backtracking down paths they'd already traversed, Matthew snapped a picture at each intersection—which turned out to be a good idea, since more than once they followed one fork, then another, and suddenly found themselves back at the first one.

Not long after lunch, the path they'd been following led them back to the house, emerging in the back garden on the second-from-right trail. "You were right about it going around in a circle," Cass said.

They'd decided since it was only one o'clock that they'd try one more trail, the second-from-left fork. Just like the first one, this too was intersected with other paths, some of which they'd already traversed down. Close to the house, some of these trails led to gardens like the dilapidated rose garden Cass had found on her first night in town; but farther out, any clearings they encountered were just patches of overgrown grass that could be natural or something man-made that had been abandoned long ago.

Either way, there was no sign of anything out of the ordinary anywhere. Cass hadn't even noticed many fae around today, and her skin had been decidedly goosebump-free—apart from those times when Matthew got too close to her, and Cass had a sneaking suspicion that her reaction had little to do with her so-called faery blessing and everything to do with Matthew.

As if it's not bad enough that he's basically the hottest guy alive, Cass thought to herself when they reached a part of the trail too narrow for them to walk side by side, and Matthew instinctively moved in front of her with Tucker, as if to look out for any potential dangers that may lay ahead—giving her, once again, an unobstructed view from behind, of which she doggedly refused to take advantage. *It's that he's basically the* perfect *guy. Nice, smart, funny,* and *he knows about fae and believes in faery blessings?*

Fate was a cruel mistress.

"It's a little bit steep up ahead," Matthew said, stopping to look over his shoulder at her. Cass peered past him and saw that the trail did indeed slope downward at a somewhat sharp angle, made worse by the presence of tangled roots poking out of the dirt and curling blackberry vines covered with thorns. Although the property was dilapidated in many parts, most of the trails were pretty clear, leading Cass to believe Alexandra was still either walking the property herself or having a gardener tend the trails up until shortly before her death. But this trail had clearly not been used in some time.

"Should we turn back?" Matthew asked.

Cass hesitated. She didn't relish the idea of tramping through those thorns; but on the other hand, what if the fact that this trail was so clearly unused was a sign that they were close to the warren? If Alexandra had had a gardener tending the other trails, maybe she'd had them avoid this one to keep them from disturbing it.

"Let's keep going," she said at last.

They picked their way cautiously down the slope. Tucker seemed to be having an easier time of it than the humans, trailing ahead of them as far as his leash would allow and then stopping to look back at Cass and Matthew, his stub tail wagging cheerfully.

They were about halfway down when Cass's stomach began to twist in warning. She stopped abruptly at the sensation. Matthew glanced back at her. "You okay?" he asked.

"Yeah," she said, trying to sort out what the feeling was trying to tell her. Were they in danger? Or did this just mean that the warren was close?

She took one more step forward. As she did, she caught a glimmer of movement near her feet, a streak of green. And then her foot caught in a thorny tendril of blackberry and she stumbled.

Matthew dropped Tucker's leash and lunged forward to steady her, but his own quick motion threw him off balance and when Cass tumbled into him, their feet tangled. The two of them tripped and stumbled down the slope, Cass's feet falling out from under her, her hip painfully impacting the rocky slope. They skidded a few feet before sliding to a stop near the bottom of the slope, a cloud of dust rising off the trail.

Cass's heart was pounding so hard that it felt like a few moments before her ears stopped ringing and her brain caught up. She blinked a few times to get her bearings. Tucker was leaping around them in circles, barking and frantically nudging them with his snout.

"It's all right, buddy," Matthew said, his voice shaky. He reached out a hand to stroke the dog, who licked his fingers. "We're all right." He turned to Cass. "Well, I think we are. Are you okay?"

Cass took a shuddering breath and tried to assess herself. She was covered in scratches and scrapes, and her hip was definitely bruised from the angle at which she'd fallen; but nothing seemed broken or too badly damaged. "I'm okay. Are you?"

Matthew nodded and laughed sheepishly. "So much for my smooth attempt at catching you."

Cass laughed as well. "You did great. I'm just sorry I dragged you down with me." As her senses caught up with her, she noticed his proximity to her on the side of the slope, their legs still brushing against each other. The way his face hovered just over hers, close enough to touch. Before she knew what she was doing, she'd reached out and put her hand on his cheek. "You've got dirt on your nose," she said quietly, brushing it off with her thumb.

His golden-brown eyes held hers a moment longer. Then he

leaned down and kissed her.

Emotions erupted inside of Cass like fireworks as his lips met hers, spreading from her stomach and rippling throughout her, warmth coursing through her veins. Somewhere, far off in the back of her mind, she remembered the dream. The love and trust and familiarity that had consumed her dream self when Matthew was beside her. But now it was amplified. It was like the dream had been a mirror reflecting this moment—beautiful but distant. As strong as she'd thought the feelings in her dream had been, they were nothing compared to now. She pulled him closer, her arms wrapping around his neck, the kiss deepening, and she realized with certainty that she never wanted to let him go. That realization hit her harder than the impact from their tumble down the slope. She was falling, falling, crashing...

Crash.

Abruptly she broke away from him. He blinked in confusion as she disentangled herself from him, jumping to her feet and brushing the dirt off her knees. Her legs wobbled, still unsteady, but she resisted the urge to sit back down.

"Cass," Matthew said, regaining his voice. "What's wrong? Are you okay?"

"I'm sorry," she said, staggering the rest of the way down the slope. "I can't. I'm sorry."

"Wait, Cass." Matthew stood, reaching out a hand toward her. "Let's talk about this."

"I'm sorry," she cried again, her voice breaking on the last syllable. She took off at a run down the trail. She didn't know where it led, but she couldn't think about it now. She couldn't think. She couldn't *stay*. If she stayed near him a moment longer, she knew she wouldn't be able to leave. And she had to. She *had* to.

For his sake.

She heard Matthew calling out to her as she ran, heard Tucker's barking grow more distant. But she didn't look back.

Chapter 14

To her relief, the trail led back to the main crossroads without any other forks to confuse her. She ran back to the house, but she didn't go inside. She didn't want to hear if he rang the doorbell, didn't want to see him drive away. Instead she hid in the solarium like the coward she was, slumping into a wicker chair between two enormous potted plants—a bit on the shriveled side, since she hadn't been the best at remembering Connie's instructions to water them—and praying she wasn't visible through the large clear glass windows that encased the sunroom.

She pulled her knees up to her chest and buried her face in them, her shoulders shaking with the force of her sobs. *Why did I do that?* she thought over and over, although she wasn't sure what the source of her regret was. Going out into the woods with Matthew at all, even though she'd known her own growing feelings for him were a problem? Touching his face like that? Kissing him back?

Or running away from what her heart so intensely longed for?

Her head was pounding by the time her tears ran out, and she was starting to get cold. She'd left her cardigan in Matthew's hiking backpack, so all she had was her short-sleeved T-shirt. She lifted her head, noticing that the sunlight reflecting into the solarium had turned orange. It was almost sunset. Matthew surely had left by now. There was no way he could have gotten lost; the trail led right back to her aunt's house. She considered going to look and see if his truck was gone, but the thought of accidentally running into him again after the way she'd just acted was too humiliating. She couldn't face him again, not after that. Even if she found some way to explain it, just *seeing* him would be painful to her.

The sound of approaching footsteps made her freeze, and she shrank deeper into the plush cushion on the wicker seat. But then the source of the footsteps entered the solarium. It was Lily, smiling cheerfully.

"Hey, Ms. Cass," she said, waving. Then, as her eyes adjusted and she took Cass's disheveled appearance in, she asked in alarm, "Are you all right?"

Cass cleared her throat, wiping her face quickly with the back of her hand. "I'm fine. I just tripped earlier."

"Oh no! Did you hurt yourself?" Lily asked, coming over to sit on the floor near Cass's feet and looking up at her.

"No," Cass replied quickly. "Did you have fun at Wildlife Safari?"

"It was so much fun! They had giraffes and zebras and elephants—and you won't believe how many fae I saw! They were playing with the animals! I wish I could have told Amelia about it."

Cass was only half listening, but she gave Lily a sharp look at that. "You haven't said anything to her about your abilities, have you?"

Lily rolled her eyes in annoyance. "No. I already told you I didn't. But I don't think it's fair, Ms. Cass! All your friends know. Ms. Emma and Ms. Hudson and Mr. McCarthy—"

At the sound of Matthew's name, Cass visibly winced. She didn't mean to; it was an involuntary reaction, but Lily caught it all the same.

"Are you sure you're all right?" Lily asked.

"I'm fine," Cass snapped, more harshly than she meant to. "Seriously, Lily," she added, trying to deflect the subject away from herself, Matthew, or, heaven forbid, herself *and* Matthew, "you can't tell Amelia."

Lily refused to be deterred. "What happened today? Did you find the warren?"

Cass shook her head, getting to her feet and pushing past Lily to go stand by the window. Her foot brushed Lily's knee as she went by. She peered out into the yard, but couldn't see her driveway from here. "Did you see if there was a truck parked in the drive when you got here?"

Lily didn't answer for a long moment. Finally, quietly, she

whispered, "Why?"

Cass glanced over at her, brows furrowed. "Why what?"

Lily sniffled, and to Cass's shock a tear slipped down the little girl's face before she could wipe it away. "Why did you run?"

Cass stared at Lily, her jaw dropped. "Lily, did you read my thoughts?"

"You love him, Ms. Cass," Lily said softly. "Why are you hurting him? And yourself?"

Cass felt like she'd been slapped. When she finally regained her voice, she snapped, "It's rude to invade people's minds like that, Lily."

The girl crossed her arms and glared back. "It's probably rude to see people's futures, too, but you can't help that, either."

Her first instinct was to tell Lily to get out. But when she opened her mouth to do so, she found she couldn't get it to form the words. Her anger melted. She was too tired to be angry at her. Especially since her words were all true. She was tired. So tired of all of this. She went back to the wicker chair and sank into it.

"Please tell me, Ms. Cass," Lily murmured into the silence. "I'm not a little kid. You can tell me."

Cass sighed, squeezing her eyes shut. "A long time ago..." she finally said, her voice thick. Her eyes stung, and she took a deep breath to keep more tears from leaking out. "A long time ago, I was engaged. That means I was supposed to get married."

"I know," Lily said.

Cass nodded. "But my fiancé... he didn't believe in fae or the Sight."

"Did you tell him?" Lily asked.

"That's not important, okay?" Cass snapped, but then she sighed. "I did tell him eventually. I had a premonition that something bad was going to happen. A lot of times when I get the premonitions, I just get a bad feeling in my stomach and I don't know what it means. But sometimes I'll get a stronger one, one that actually shows me what will happen."

She opened her eyes, looking at Lily. The girl was watching attentively.

"That night I had a dream. I dreamed that if Jeremy—my fiancé—if he took his motorcycle out that day, he'd get into an accident. I was really worried, so I told him." She swallowed. "He didn't believe me, even after I explained to him about my Sight. In fact, when I told him that, he laughed in my face. He told me I was being ridiculous. So he went out on his bike. And sure enough... he went off the road on the Angeles Crest Highway."

Cass closed her eyes, remembering the way her heart had dropped out from under her when Jeremy's mom had called and told her he'd been in an accident. The despair that had overwhelmed her, because she'd *warned* him and he had just laughed. He hadn't believed. Just like everyone else, he hadn't believed. And it had nearly killed him.

"It was a miracle that he didn't die," she said, "but he was paralyzed from the waist down. And... he blamed me. When he was finally awake in the hospital, when he saw me, he told me to get away from him. That I was a freak. I thought, okay, he's upset. I'll just give him some time to process it. I tried going back a few times, but he just got angrier every time he saw me. So finally... I gave him back his ring. Emma kept insisting that he just needed more time. That he'd call when he came to his senses. But he never called."

In the months following the accident, she'd blamed herself even more than Jeremy had blamed her. What was the good of having an ability like this if no one believed you? It would be better not to know at all. She'd spent agonizing hours wondering if her warning had done more harm than good. Had he been more reckless, more cocky, in an attempt to show her and her stupid premonitions wrong?

"But Mr. McCarthy isn't like that," Lily said quietly. "He believes in the fae, and he believes in our gifts. If you told him, he wouldn't ignore you. He'd probably be extra careful to do what you told him."

"And what if it didn't help? What if the stuff he did to be more careful wound up being the thing that put him in danger to begin with?" Cass asked. "Then I would still have caused him to get hurt."

"But what if your warning would actually save him?" Lily countered fiercely. "What if the whole point of your power is to be able to help people, and what's hurting them is the fact that you're keeping everything secret?"

"You don't understand," Cass said, her voice rising angrily. "You're just a kid, Lily. You don't get how the world works."

"You're just being selfish!" Lily snapped, jumping to her feet and putting her hands on her hips. "You're telling yourself you're doing this to protect him, but you're just trying to protect your own feelings. You think if you don't let yourself love anybody, then *you* won't get hurt if something bad happens. But that's just being a selfish brat. And you think that you can fix my powers by teaching me to be selfish, too. But I would rather hear everyone's thoughts forever, no matter how loud they are, than be as selfish as you are!"

Cass stared at her, dumbstruck. Lily's words felt like a physical blow. "Fine," she said slowly, standing and walking over to the solarium door. "Obviously you know more about this than I do. So you won't need lessons from me anymore, will you?"

Lily stood silent, her eyes locked on Cass. "Are you kicking me out?" she asked at last.

"I'm just saying you obviously don't need help from me."

Lily stared at her a moment longer. "You're going to leave, aren't you?"

Cass bristled. "Are you reading my thoughts again?"

"I don't have to," Lily spat. "Anyone could see what you're thinking. Don't you care at all about what's going to happen to the woods if you leave?"

Cass squared her shoulders. "Not really."

Lily's mouth opened, but no response came. She stared at Cass a moment longer, then squeezed her eyes shut and shoved past her through the solarium door, down the steps into the backyard, disappearing between the trees.

Cass watched her, struggling to keep from calling out to Lily to come back. It was too late for that. None of this could be fixed. Cass had broken it beyond repair.

All I wanted was to keep him safe, she thought. But that was a lie, wasn't it? She *was* only trying to protect herself. Her own feelings. To keep her own heart from breaking again, the way it had when Jeremy had hurled his poisonous words at her. She'd spent five years telling herself she was unlovable. She *believed* she was unlovable. She still believed it. One of these days, Matthew would realize that, and she knew with absolute conviction that when Matthew broke her heart, it would be a thousand times worse than when Jeremy had done it.

Her eyes came back into focus as she noticed movement in the trees. She thought for an instant that Lily had come back, but then she saw the flash of chartreuse between the branches. And she remembered the glimmer she'd caught out of the corner of her eye just before she fell on the trail.

"Did you trip me earlier?" she asked, glaring at Green as he watched her from the trees. "Trying to get another reaction?"

"I don't know you anymore," Green said, ignoring her

question.

Cass rolled her eyes. "You never knew me to begin with."

"I thought I did," Green replied, his voice quiet and lilting like a mourning dove. "What happened to you? What happened to the girl you used to be?"

Cass's skin prickled at his words. She ran a hand over her bare arms, chilled in the cool evening air. "Life happened," she said.

Green shook his head sadly. "You're the cause of your own misery." With that, he disappeared into the trees.

"I know," Cass whispered to the empty air.

Chapter 15

Cass's cardigan was folded neatly on the mat on the front porch. Matthew's truck was nowhere to be seen. She sighed as she picked the sweater up and reached for the doorknob, but paused when something blue fluttered out of the folds of fabric in her hand. Her stomach turned as she recognized it as a tarot card. Slowly she crouched, picking the card up from the floor.

The illustration showed a bright yellow orb in the sky, two dogs—or maybe wolves?—baying at it. The caption beneath it read *The Moon*.

The sight of this new card reminded her of the other card she'd found weeks ago, the one on the servant's stairs. She'd forgotten all about it. She'd never asked Emma about its meaning; there had been so much else on her mind, what with learning that Lily had the Sight and that Aunt Alexandra had been teaching her, that Cass had just shoved it into her nightstand drawer with the other two cards.

She went into the house, where she was greeted by Onyx screaming for his dinner. After dishing up a saucer of wet food for him, she went up to her room and pulled the stack of cards out, laying them on her bed and adding the newest one to the set. She didn't want to call Emma. Em was too good at reading Cass's emotions. She'd immediately want to know what was wrong, and she'd immediately figure out that it had something to do with Matthew McCarthy, and she'd probably give Cass the same lecture that she'd just been given by a nine-year-old child.

Instead, Cass pulled her phone out of her pocket and did a quick Google search. She started with the card she'd found tonight, *The Moon.*

The Moon reflects your fears, read the first website she encountered. *Oftentimes these fears stem from something that occurred in the past, a traumatic experience you are afraid of reliving. The Moon frequently appears during a time of uncertainty. It urges you not to make a hasty decision, particularly one based on fear.*

Cass swallowed and set the card aside, reaching for the one she'd found on the servants' stairs. It was the *Ace of Cups.*

The Ace of Cups is a symbol of pure love. Love is in your heart, overflowing from within you. It's time for you to give it freely. When the Ace of Cups appears in a reading, it oftentimes foretells of the beginning of a new relationship, be it a romantic one or a blossoming friendship.

The phone shook in Cass's hand.

"If I were to leave you a card, it certainly wouldn't be that *one."* Green's voice echoed in Cass's head, high and reedy and mocking. Maybe he really *did* know her.

Tears were biting at her eyes again. Cass squeezed them shut and flung the phone down on her bed.

Cass spent the next two days cleaning and purging with extreme prejudice. She'd made her mind up: she was leaving. She'd shoved all those stupid cards into a drawer and vowed not to think of them again. She didn't know what kind of life the person, creature, or entity who was leaving her the cards seemed to think she had, but she knew that it wasn't for her, and certainly not now. She told the little voice in her head that was urging her to heed the advice of *The Moon* to *shut up*, and first thing Sunday morning, she'd called Mr. Kowalski.

"I'm not going to be ready to sign anything until all of my aunt's affairs are settled," she'd reminded him. But yes, she'd told him, once everything was taken care of, the house and the grounds were his.

Her stomach had immediately begun twisting itself into knots, and all day Sunday her skin erupted into gooseflesh at least once an hour. But she ignored it. The decision was made. The fae could shriek and complain and generally try to make her miserable all they wanted, but it wasn't her problem. She knew as soon as she was out of Riddle and back in a nice, civilized urban setting, everything would be better. And she decided she'd about had enough of the West Coast. It was time to try somewhere else on for size. New York would probably be a good option. She seriously doubted she'd run into any supernatural creatures there.

She wouldn't leave Riddle completely high and dry, of course. The idea had come to her in the night: the warren could still be protected. She just had to find it. Once that was done, she could add a provision to her sales contract that Kowalski would need to leave it and a small greenbelt around it untouched. If he tried to protest that, she would go to the Riddle City Council and request that they designate that area protected. Kowalski would still have plenty of room for his mammoth development. So what if he had to build four hundred and eighty houses instead of an even five hundred. He'd still be rolling in dough by the time they all sold.

It made total sense. A good compromise that would make everyone happy.

So why was she so miserable about it?

Monday morning she woke up feeling like she'd been run over by a bulldozer. She hadn't slept so badly since the first night she'd been here. The nightmare about Lily and the warren replayed on a loop in her brain every time she managed to doze off. The dream was the same as it had always been, but somehow it felt worse, particularly after the argument she'd had with the girl. Just one more example of Cass ruining everything she touched.

She didn't have work that day, so she spent the morning boxing up books and lugging them into the entryway to carry out to her car. Sometime around noon, when she staggered down the front steps, struggling under the weight of the first banker's box full of hardbacks, she heard a sound in the distance like a lawnmower.

Several hours later, Cass was sweating and exhausted and her sedan was packed as full of boxes as she could get it while still fitting in the driver's seat herself. She leaned against the closed trunk, breathing out a sigh and wiping her brow. In the distance, the lawnmower was still running, though it was past three o'clock now. Someone with a big property must be manicuring their lawn. It sounded too far away to be the Fischers, though. Maybe the Kowalskis?

She looked up at the sound of a car and saw the white van of the post office driving away from the mailboxes on the opposite side of the street. She glanced around cautiously. No sign of Connie. Might as well grab the mail while it was safe. She'd done a good job of hiding from her nosy neighbor since Matthew's arrival on Saturday, and she had no intention of breaking that streak.

She should have known that her luck wouldn't hold out. Just as she reached her box, Connie came springing out of her front door like a jack-in-the-box. She'd probably been waiting at her front window for just this occasion.

Cass tried to avoid eye contact, pulling her mail quickly out of her aunt's purple box. "Hi, Mrs. Fischer," she said when Connie appeared beside her.

"I hope you're happy," Connie said.

This wasn't the reaction Cass had been expecting. She'd anticipated a grilling about what Matthew McCarthy had been doing at her house all day Saturday, not immediate, outright antagonism.

"I'm sorry?" Cass said.

"How much did he give you?" Connie asked, her dark brows furrowed angrily over her green eyes.

Cass blinked. "How much did who—"

"Kowalski," Connie snapped, her perm whipping around her face. "Your devil's deal with Tom Kowalski."

Cass grimaced. Word about that had already gone out? What had Kowalski done, called a town meeting to gloat about it? Considering the story Darcy had told Cass on her first day of work, maybe that wasn't completely far-fetched...

"We haven't signed any papers yet," Cass said noncommittally, hoping her words would soothe her neighbor's temper. But instead, Connie laughed derisively.

"Oh, is that so?" Connie scoffed.

"It is so," Cass said through clenched teeth.

"Well, maybe you ought to remind Tom of that, then. Since his construction crew is down on the edge of your property ripping trees out."

Cass stared at Connie, dumbfounded. "Excuse me?"

"Right down at the end of the road," Connie said, thrusting her arm in the direction the lawnmower sound was coming from, her bracelets jangling. "They've been at it all day. And if you're telling the truth that you haven't signed anything yet, then you better go put a stop to it, because I know that several of those trees they pulled down are past your property line."

Cass stared at her a moment longer, the noise she'd been hearing all morning ringing in her ears, her brain slowly processing that she wasn't hearing a mower—she was hearing heavy machinery. She slammed her box closed and ran down the street as fast as her legs could carry her, a stack of mail clenched tightly in her right hand.

Sure enough, at the edge of where her property bordered the Kowalskis', a giant yellow excavator was gripping a skinny pine between the teeth of its claw. As Cass stared in horror, the machine pulled the tree out like it was nothing more than a weed, its roots dropping dirt like a waterfall. The excavator dumped the pine onto a disturbingly large pile of already-felled trees.

Her stomach roiled. She had to squeeze her eyes shut and take several deep breaths through her nose to keep from heaving. She would never have expected the sight of felled trees to make her feel so sick, but something about it... it was like walking in on the scene of a massacre. The air smelled metallic, almost bloody. She could feel the anger and pain of the woods in the very air around her. The rage of the fae.

"Our retribution will be swift."

"Stop!" Cass screamed to be heard over the sound of the machinery. The excavator, of course, did *not* stop. She noticed a man in a hard hat with a reflective vest standing near the tree line directing the driver of the machine, so she raced forward, nearly colliding with him as she skidded to a stop on the freshly turned earth.

The man in the hard hat looked at her in confusion, then gestured for the driver of the excavator to turn it off.

"What are you doing?" Cass yelled once it was quiet. The noise from the machinery still rang in her ears.

"Just doing some clearing for Cow Creek Development," the man replied cheerfully.

"You're on *my* land," Cass protested, waving a clothing catalog and a stack of credit card solicitations in his face.

"I don't think so," said the man, his smile wavering.

"You *are*," Cass replied firmly. "I haven't signed any papers yet."

"I understand that, ma'am, but according to Mr. Kowalski, these trees are over his property line. He wanted to get work started on the parcel he already owns."

"He *doesn't* own this," Cass argued. "This is my property!"

"You're going to need a surveyor to confirm that, ma'am," said the worker, "and until then, I'm not authorized to stop work."

Cass gawked at him. "So you're just going to keep cutting trees down even though the ownership of this land is contested?"

"Orders are orders."

"I'm sorry, are Kowalski's orders a royal decree?" Cass snapped. When he just blinked at her, Cass rolled her eyes. "What happens if it turns out that the surveyor confirms that this *is* my property and all the trees have already been torn down?"

"Well, that's above my pay grade," said the man. "But I assume that in that case, you'd need to file suit for a cash settlement."

"A cash settlement isn't going to bring the trees back!" Cass protested.

The man shrugged at her. "I don't know what you're so upset about. The trees are coming down once you sell your property, anyway."

Cass's stomach churned again, even more violently than before. She squeezed her eyes shut once more as the man waved to the excavator and the horrible sound of machinery filled the air around her like the roar of a tsunami.

She started to walk back down to the sidewalk, but after a couple steps her knees buckled and she sank to the ground, her skin crawling like she had an army of ants climbing all over her, her stomach lurching and heaving. Her vision swam and clouded, and suddenly an image appeared in her mind, as clear as if she were looking at a video on her phone. Tom Kowalski sitting at a large, modern desk made of dark gray wood. The room he was in was brightly illuminated, monochrome apart from the blue sky through the picture window behind the desk. A utilitarian lamp glowed on the desk before him, like a spotlight on the atrocity playing out. He was gasping for breath, choking, clawing at his throat.

He couldn't see the long, spindly fingers of the fae wrapped around his throat. Couldn't see the sinister grins on their narrow, pointed faces as he struggled for air.

The vision cleared, and Cass jerked alert. The fistful of mail had dropped from her hands when her knees gave out and was currently splayed across the upturned earth like evidence from a crime scene, but she paid it no mind. Abandoning the papers, she ran back to the man in the hard hat.

"Where is Mr. Kowalski?" she shouted at the top of her lungs.

"What?"

"Where is he right now?" she screamed.

"I think he's working from his home office today," the man in the hard hat yelled back at her. She could tell by the expression he was giving her what he was thinking: that she was planning on tracking him down and chewing him out for encroaching on her property. And she definitely would be doing that—later.

First, she needed to save his life.

Chapter 16

The Kowalski property was essentially the polar opposite of Alexandra's. Though situated on several acres, there was hardly a tree to be seen—only neatly manicured hedges and blunt-topped arborvitaes forming a wall around the house. The home itself was a Mediterranean-style two-story faced in peach-colored stucco, with a red tile roof. The flat face of the building was broken up by huge windows that reflected the green lawn and blue sky back at Cass. She ran as fast as she could across the brick driveway and up the three steps to the front door.

She rang the doorbell, pressing the button down repeatedly as though that would make whoever was inside answer more quickly. For a panicked moment she feared that there was no one home but Mr. Kowalski, and if that were the case, it may be too late. But to her relief, after a minute the door swung open. A tiny, harried-looking woman with black hair cut in a sleek pixie style blinked up at Cass. "What?" she asked.

"Is Mr. Kowalski at home?" Cass asked, struggling for breath. She knew she must look and sound like a maniac, but there wasn't time to worry about appearances right now.

"He's busy," the woman said, looking annoyed.

"This is an emergency. Where's his office?" She pushed past the woman, who spluttered with outrage.

"Excuse you! You can't just come barging your way into my house!"

My house, she said. So this must be Mrs. Kowalski. Darcy hadn't been kidding about the age gap between Lily's parents. She supposed this woman probably must be in her thirties, or close to it; but her looks and demeanor combined to make her seem younger. Practically like a college student.

"I'm sorry, but I need to see Mr. Kowalski immediately," Cass said. "Where is his office?"

The woman simply sputtered some more. Cass didn't have time for this. In her vision, the view through the picture window was definitely a ground floor vantage. It was hard to tell from the austere landscaping, but she assumed the office would probably be near the back of the house for privacy's sake, and she dashed across the marbled entryway and down the closest hallway in search of it. A set of double doors stood at the end of the hall. Breathlessly, Cass flung them open.

The stark office looked just as it had in Cass's vision. Hardwood floor stained a dull gray against off-white walls, black or dark gray accents everywhere giving it an austere, modern look. Not a splash of color to be seen except through the picture window and through a slightly-ajar set of French doors on the wall to Cass's right.

And, of course, around Kowalski's neck.

"Stop!" Cass cried, rushing across the room. Kowalski was no longer struggling the way he'd been in her vision. He was slumped over in his black leather office chair. He looked to be unconscious. She prayed that that was *all* he was.

The fae were cackling to themselves until Cass reached them. She grabbed the two imps, clutching one in each fist, and ripped them off his chest, where they'd been dancing a victory jig. Her hands burned from their magic, but she didn't loosen her grip. As they screamed in protest, she marched over to the open French door and hurled them out. "And don't come back!" she shouted, slamming the door in their faces. Then she whirled back to Kowalski and quickly checked his vital signs. He wasn't breathing.

"What's wrong with him?" his wife screeched from the doorway. She'd followed behind Cass, but at a much more dignified pace, so Cass was relatively certain that she hadn't witnessed the faery removal. She hoped not, at least. If Mrs. Kowalski didn't have the Sight—and everything Lily had ever said had indicated that neither of her parents did—then Cass definitely would have looked like a lunatic.

"Call 9-1-1," Cass barked at her over her shoulder. She rolled his chair away from his desk, catching Kowalski's body against her shoulder as he slumped forward. She eased him down onto the floor, laying him flat on his back and unbuttoning the top button of his shirt to loosen his collar. She'd had her last public employee CPR recertification less than a year ago, but would she remember all the steps?

"What's wrong with him?" Mrs. Kowalski repeated.

"He's not breathing!" Cass snapped back. "Call 9-1-1!"

She took a deep breath, pinched his nostrils shut with her fingers, and leaned forward.

The paramedics arrived quickly. They loaded Mr. Kowalski onto a gurney and rushed him out of the house. One of them asked Cass what happened, and she told them the closest version of the truth that she could offer: that she'd come over, angry, to confront him about his workers encroaching on her property line, and found him unconscious at his desk. The paramedics and Mrs. Kowalski seemed to accept this, though she wouldn't be surprised if she had to answer to the police later. That would be fine, she tried to assure herself. She certainly hadn't been alone in the room with him long enough to have choked him out herself. Mrs. Kowalski had arrived just seconds after her and found Cass already preparing to administer rescue breathing.

"Could this day get any worse?" Mrs. Kowalski wailed as she watched the paramedics loading her husband into the ambulance. "First Lily and now Tom?"

Cass felt like her blood had turned to ice water. The chill that washed over her was instantaneous, making her shiver. "What about Lily?"

"She's run away!" Mrs. Kowalski cried, wiping her nose with the cuff of her sweater.

Cass was too stunned by her words to wince at that. "What do you mean, she's run away?"

"Her school called just before you got here to say she was absent today. I thought she may have played hooky, gone off with that little homeschooled friend of hers, but I just got off the phone with her parents and they said they hadn't seen her since Saturday." She narrowed her eyes at Cass. "Wait. You're the one who owns Alexandra's property now, aren't you? She hasn't been at your house today, has she?"

Cass shook her head. She felt sick. Absolutely sick. Like if she didn't sit down right now, she was going to throw up or pass out. Possibly both. "I haven't seen her since Saturday, either," she said, her voice rough.

"I don't know what to do," Mrs. Kowalski whimpered. "I don't want Tom to be alone at the hospital, but what if Lily comes home and no one is here?"

Cass didn't think she would, not based on the crawling

sensation she was feeling across her skin. She had a strong suspicion she knew where Lily had gone, and it wasn't somewhere that Mrs. Kowalski could follow.

"You go with your husband," she said. "I'll look for Lily."

Mrs. Kowalski easily agreed—the cynical side of Cass wondered if this was small-town trust of neighbors or simply silly, young Mrs. Kowalski eager to pass her responsibility on to *anyone* else—and gave Cass her cell phone number to call if Lily returned or if Cass heard anything. Cass watched mutely as she ran to the garage at the end of the brick driveway and drove out a moment later in a shiny black BMW X model.

As the car disappeared down the drive, Cass heard movement in the hedges behind her. She turned to see Green watching her from between the thick, scaly leaves of the arborvitaes. Before Cass could react, he murmured, "I tried to warn you."

Cass stared at him. "What?"

"Time and time again I tried to warn you. But you wouldn't listen. And now it may be too late."

"Do you know where Lily is?" Cass asked frantically. But in the blink of an eye, Green had disappeared.

Chapter 17

She'd been spirited away. That was the only possible explanation. The fae were taking their revenge on Kowalski.

But not just him. Cass knew that. The fae were punishing her, too. It was supposed to be her job to protect the woods. To be the Chatelaine. And she'd turned her back on them. She'd told herself that what happened to Riddle wasn't her problem. She had no ties holding her here, no reason to stay. No reason to give up her dreams just to appease some ancient agreement that she hadn't been a part of and didn't need to be beholden to.

The fae had shown her just how wrong she was.

Now the meaning of her dream was so agonizingly clear, and it was too late to stop it. *"We'll all die."* The fae had almost killed Tom Kowalski—would have, if Cass hadn't been there to stop them. And now they had Lily. Would the fae be satisfied with a sacrifice of the entire Kowalski family? Or would their wrath spread to the whole of Riddle? Would they go after Darcy next?

Would they go after Matthew?

Cass had caused this, and it was only now in sickening retrospect that she could see what a selfish monster she'd been. Just like Lily had said. After Jeremy's accident, she'd been so hurt that she let the hurt change her, all the while denying it to the moon. And what had been the point? Had she been trying to protect others, as she'd convinced herself? Or just trying to protect herself?

Regardless, it had backfired miserably. She'd told herself that she didn't care what happened to Riddle, but now that she was here, she realized that she did care, very much. There were people here that she cared about, more than she'd cared about anyone in years. She'd made friends in this small town, found people who cared about her for who she was. People she didn't have to keep secrets with. And now one of those people was in danger.

There still had to be time to stop this. Maybe it wasn't too late to save Lily.

And everyone else in the process.

Cass raced back up the street to her house. She knew she could get onto her property from the Kowalskis' side, but she didn't know her way around the woods well enough to trust she wouldn't get lost, and she didn't have time for that right now. This was an emergency and every second counted.

As she passed the place where the construction crew had been working, she saw that they'd left, but the excavator still stood near where she'd seen it last, its yellow arm crooked in the sky like a giant bent tree. It was a stark reminder of the real trees that had stood in that very spot hours before, but now lay piled in an unceremonious heap yards away. The workers must have been given the order to stop for the day—they'd probably figured they should get going while the going was good when they'd noticed the flashing lights of the ambulance and fire engine on their boss's driveway—but the machine's lingering presence showed they obviously thought they'd be back, possibly as soon as tomorrow.

Not if Cass had anything to say about it.

She raced down the sidewalk-less shoulder of the road but careened to a stop when she turned onto her driveway and saw a silver pickup parked there.

She struggled to catch her breath. "Matthew," she said.

He'd been leaning against the open bed of the truck, but he straightened when he saw her. An indescribable tumult of emotions washed over Cass at the sight of him. She wanted to run, but she couldn't say whether she wanted to run away from him... or toward him.

"Hey," Matthew said. When she didn't respond—her mouth was moving, but no sound would come—he quickly added, "Look, I know I'm probably not real welcome here. I realize from your reaction on Saturday that I obviously misunderstood—"

"No, no," Cass blurted. Hearing him say that was like a knife jabbing her heart. He hadn't misunderstood. Not by a *long* shot.

He waved her off. "That's not important. I wouldn't ordinarily come harassing a girl who made her feelings clear like that. But Lily wasn't in class today, and then I just..." He shrugged helplessly. "I had a feeling. You know, like the ones I told you about. I had a feeling that I needed to be here."

He took a step closer, his expression so vulnerable that Cass's heart ached all over again. "Was I wrong?" he asked.

"You weren't wrong." She swallowed and shook her head. "About that, anyway. We do need to talk, Matthew. I need to apologize. But later. Right now, we have to save Lily."

Matthew nodded grimly. "So, I was right, then? She's here? And in danger?"

"I think so. Matthew, I think... I think the fae have her. And it's all my fault."

He sucked in a breath. "Do you know where she's at?" he asked.

"I think she must be at the warren."

"So we have to find it, then," Matthew said.

She nodded, and without hesitation she and Matthew ran to the place where the garden paths converged.

"It could be down either of these trails," Matthew said, looking around at the forked crossroads before them. "We didn't check either of these on Saturday. You said you already tried this one, right?" He gestured to the path Cass had taken her first evening in Riddle.

"Right," she started to say, but then she froze. Had she seen it just now? A glimmer of light and color. A flash of green.

"You need to watch yourself."

She remembered the sound of music and the ring of light. She'd been pixy-led that night, been so embarrassed that the fae had been able to trick her like that when they never had before. She'd been annoyed with herself for letting her guard down, but what if the reason they'd been able to take hold of her like that was because the fae were stronger there? Like they would be if, for example, they were close to a power source?

Such as a portal through the veil...

"I'm an idiot," she muttered.

"What?" said Matthew.

"It's down there," Cass said, pointing down the trail with certainty. "The warren is down this path. I'm an idiot for not seeing it before. They were misleading me." *They were probably angry that I kicked that brownie out,* she thought. *My first act of thumbing my nose at the role of Chatelaine.* Her behavior since arriving in Riddle had done nothing but disrupt the balance of the wood, a balance that had been in place for over a century, since Mrs. Porter had taken on her role as caretaker. No wonder Cass's premonitory senses had been so overloaded as long as she'd been here. The balance was disrupted—and she was the one who had done it.

There has to still be time to restore the balance, she thought.

"Let's go," she said to Matthew. He nodded, and the two of them raced down the trail.

It felt like they ran and ran, but the end of the trail was nowhere in sight. The light between the trees seemed to change, becoming more golden, glowing orange. Or was it an optical illusion, caused by the changing leaves above their heads? As her legs pumped and her breath came out raggedly, Cass found herself continually reminded of how much time she'd lost when last she came down this path. Two hours gone looking at the moon. If the warren was a portal between worlds, what would it do to time and space around it? What if they really were running for eternity, time passing around them while they didn't move, the trees around them staying stationary?

Then, suddenly, the trees parted and they burst into a clearing. The sky above was the purple of twilight. It couldn't have been later than four o'clock when Cass found Matthew on the driveway. Had they really been running for three hours? Or was it another faery illusion, like the glowing ring of the moon? Cass's skin rippled with gooseflesh and her stomach twisted into knots.

In the center of the clearing was an enormous oak tree, the largest one Cass had ever seen. Its branches formed a canopy that encased almost the whole clearing, and they seemed to stretch high enough to touch the sky. As Cass looked at it, she realized this wasn't just one tree, but two oaks who'd grown side-by-side until their trunks became so massive that they grew into each other, forming a massive entity that was cloven down the middle where they collided.

Then, as her eyes traveled down the tree, she noticed two things at once:

The clearing was crawling with fae, more than she'd ever seen in one place. They climbed up and down the body of the tree, making its bark seem to shimmer. They dangled from the branches, perched on the knobbly roots that protruded from the ground. Dozens of fae—hundreds—uncountable shades of gray and brown, bronze and gold, short and squat, long and narrow, round faces with bulbous noses and pointed faces with craggy features. They glared at Cass as one, angry eyes flashing in the gloom.

And in the center of them, in the place where the two trunks met, was Lily.

She looked like a sleeping princess in a fairy tale, her eyes closed, her expression peaceful. But she wasn't lying on a bed covered in rose petals—the bark of the tree was absorbing her, like one of those pictures of nature reclaiming objects left outside too long. All that was visible was her head and shoulders, her hands and wrists, and her feet in their anachronistic saddle shoes.

"Lily," Cass said, stepping forward, but she stopped in her tracks as the fae tensed, many of them hissing at her and crouching in decidedly antagonistic positions. They were willing to fight for their prize, it would seem.

"What can you see?" Cass whispered to Matthew.

"I see Lily," he whispered back. "Caught in the tree. I assume this is the warren?"

Cass nodded. "You can't see the fae?"

"No. Are there a lot of them?"

Cass nodded. "An army of them."

Matthew looked at her in alarm. "That doesn't sound good. Do you think they're going to try to fight you?"

The air around her was charged with energy. None of the fae moved, but they were tensed, ready to jump at a second's notice. "Probably," she said.

Matthew let out a hiss of breath. "This is nothing like Foreston. What got these fae so riled up?"

Cass swallowed. "Me."

The tree moved. Like a living creature, like a snake gradually swallowing its prey, the bark shifted and more of Lily disappeared into it. Now all that was visible was her face and the tips of her fingers on her right hand.

"Lily!" Cass screamed, darting forward without thinking. As she collided with the tree, the fae collided with her. They swarmed over her, nipping and biting her skin like rodents. She heard Matthew shout behind her. "Stay back!" she called to him. "You can't see them, so you can't fight them! They could kill you!"

She clawed at the bark, trying to find some way to break Lily out of her magical prison. The fae pulled at her hair, tore at her clothes. She could feel their hands around her throat the way they'd wrapped around Tom Kowalski's just hours before. One of them grabbed at her necklace, and then Cass heard a little squeak of pain as it dropped the chain.

The key! she thought, desperately grasping it between her fingers. *Is it iron?* She pulled it from around her neck and swung wildly at the fae nearest her. The creature screeched as the metal connected with its skin, burning it.

For a moment, Cass thought she might have the upper hand, as the fae nearest to her skittered away, eager to avoid the touch of the iron; but above her head, more fae let out angry war cries like the shrieks of eagles and dove down on her, biting at her ankles and grasping at her shirttail.

Frantically, she tried to press the iron against the bark of the tree to see if that might force it to release Lily, but it did no good. Then something bit down hard on the tender flesh of her upper arm just above her elbow. She cried out in pain, her muscles spasming, her fingers losing their grip on the key. It slipped out of her grasp to the ground. At her feet, fae skittered away from the key, but they just swarmed up her body, climbing all over her, pinning her against the tree so that she couldn't move, couldn't bend to pick the necklace up again. They had her trapped. She felt the tree convulse against her, and suddenly realized that they were planning to trap her here forever, just like Lily.

Distantly, she heard Matthew's voice behind her again, shouting her name. "Don't!" she yelled back. "Get out of here,

Matthew! You have to stay safe!"

But her words did no good. She felt his hand on her shoulders, felt more fae crawl over her and onto him, an invisible force that would surely kill Matthew the way it had almost killed Mr. Kowalski, and there was nothing Cass could do to stop it.

"You can still stop it," a voice shouted over the cacophony of shrieking fae. She recognized it—high and reedy, like a birdsong. *"You know how!"*

"I don't know how," she protested. Her voice sounded far away to her own ears. Everything was getting dark—was it night falling, or her own vision failing?

"You do! You have to remember, Cass!"

Remember? Remember what? How was she supposed to even think with a swarm of magical creatures climbing all over her body, all over Matthew, grasping and clawing and biting, pain shooting through her so intensely that even her crawling skin and churning stomach felt like a distant memory.

Her vision swam, and out of the corner of her mind's eye, she saw it—this tree, in the dappled sunlight of morning.

"That's it! Remember!"

She squeezed her eyes shut, grasping for it, and then it came to her, as strong as the vision she'd had this afternoon. But this wasn't a vision of the future—it was a memory of the past.

She and Aunt Alexandra were walking down the trail. She was

little, so small that her head only went as high as her great-aunt's hip. Alexandra held her hand tightly, guiding her over roots and rocks and other bumps on the trail. And on Alexandra's shoulder sat Green, perched like a parrot.

"Here it is," Alexandra said as they entered the clearing. "The warren."

"This is where faeries are born?" Cass asked, looking at Green hesitantly. Her childish voice was like a memory from a dream.

"Close enough," Green replied.

"Without this tree, Green and all your other friends would die," Aunt Alexandra told her. "So that's why we have to keep it safe."

"That's why you have to stay here forever?" Cass asked.

"Nobody can stay here forever," Aunt Alexandra said with a laugh. "Someone else will have to protect it someday, when I'm gone."

"I'll do it," Cass said eagerly, looking from her aunt to Green to the tree. Faeries and gnomes climbed all over its branches like a jungle gym, watching her curiously.

"Are you sure?" Alexandra asked. "It's a big responsibility."

"I'll do it!" Cass repeated. "I promise!"

Cass's vision swam again, and she was back in the present moment. The fae swarming over her had stilled, their attacks halted. They clung to her silently. Waiting.

Waiting for her to remember her promise.

She pushed away from the tree, the fae dropping off her to the ground, watching. Her knees wobbled, but Matthew caught her elbow, steadying her. Green sat on his shoulder, watching Cass.

Everyone was watching Cass.

She looked around the clearing, then back at the tree. At Lily's sleeping face peeking out through the bark. Then she sighed.

Cass crouched, placing her hands on a large, knobbly root. "I'm sorry," she said, her voice cracking. She cleared her throat and tried again. "I'm sorry for the mistakes I've made. I'm sorry I forgot." A promise made when she was too young to know what she was saying, but still binding nonetheless. A promise forgotten. Years in the human world had worn her down, stripped her of the joy she'd felt in all things magical before all the whispered jeers of her classmates and concerned eyes of adults had hardened her. She'd been so concerned about what others thought about her that she'd isolated herself in a man-made prison of concrete and iron. She'd been so desperate to forget who she really was that her mind had obliged.

But it was time to remember. To save Lily. To save Riddle.

To save the woods.

"I renew my promise," she said, her voice echoing around the clearing. "I will accept my role as caretaker of these woods. As long as I'm living, the warren and all the other trees here will be safe."

Warmth flowed from the roots of the tree into Cass's hands. The bark glowed softly, as if illuminated by a bright, full moon overhead. The fae retreated back into the branches, watching from above.

And then the trunk parted down its seam, glowing brightly, and Lily slumped forward as the tree released her. Matthew moved to catch her, lowering her to her knees as the light from the tree dissipated. A moment later, the girl's eyelashes fluttered, and her eyes slowly opened.

She looked around from Cass to Matthew to Green in confusion. "Where am I?" she asked at last, her voice thick with sleep.

"You gave us a scare there, Lily," Matthew said, grinning in relief.

"You found the warren," Cass said. "Good job."

"I did?" Lily murmured, still seeming confused. Then she blinked, her eyes focusing on Cass, and sat bolt upright.

"Ms. Cass! You didn't leave?" She slumped a little. "But you're still going to."

"No," Cass said. "I'm staying."

Lily's eyes widened. "You are?"

Cass nodded. "You were right, Lily. I'm sorry about what I said before. I was being selfish. But I want to start over. You had the right idea, kid," she said, gently stroking Lily's sleek black hair. "I'm the one who had it all wrong."

"Took you long enough to figure that one out," Green said from Matthew's shoulder.

Lily giggled and flung her arms around Cass. Cass blinked in surprise for a moment before returning the hug.

When Lily withdrew, Cass weakly got to her feet and bent down to help Lily stand. Matthew reached out a hand as well, and Lily took each, her right hand in Matthew's left and her left in Cass's right. She let out a little gasp as she straightened her knees, and Cass was about to ask if she'd hurt herself when Lily exclaimed, "Mr. McCarthy, you can see Mr. Green?"

Cass looked at Matthew in surprise. Green, still sitting on Matthew's shoulder, grinned. "I let him see me," the fae said. "I figured he'd earned it after all he's been through this last month."

Matthew nodded, turning his head to look at the creature. "He showed up right after you ran at that tree," he said to Cass. "Told me to get in there and help you, and he'd keep his friends at bay."

Cass quirked an eyebrow. "That was surprisingly forthcoming of you," Cass said.

Green shrugged modestly.

"Well, I'd say we've had quite a day." Matthew reached out a hand to steady Cass as she took a shaky step forward. "We need to check in with your mother and let her know we found you," he said to Lily, "and I think we've earned some pizza after that."

Lily let out a squeal of delight and scurried ahead on the trail, Green hopping off Matthew's shoulder to keep up with her. Cass started after them but paused as her feet kicked something in the dark. Her key necklace, still lying on the ground where it had dropped earlier. She crouched to pick it up, feeling eyes in the tree above her watching.

"You okay?" Matthew asked, looking over his shoulder at her.

She nodded, slipping the key into her pocket. "Just remembering something I almost forgot."

Chapter 18

It was seven-thirty when they got back to the house. As before, the return trip was much shorter than the journey *to* the warren. A mystery Cass suspected she'd never quite figure out.

Once inside, she called Lily's mother on her cell phone and explained that she'd found Lily hiding in the woods on her property.

"I should have known," Mrs. Kowalski said, sounding distracted. "She loves those woods too much. She hasn't been taking her father's development plans well at all. I think the three of us are going to have to sit down and have a long discussion."

Cass rolled her eyes. The time for that was probably long past.

Mr. Kowalski had regained consciousness around seven o'clock—just at the same time, Cass suspected, that she'd been swearing her fealty to the warren. There didn't seem to be anything wrong with him, so the hospital diagnosed him with respiratory distress and indicated that they'd like to keep him overnight for observation. Cass offered to bring Lily to the hospital to see her father, but Mrs. Kowalski had insisted that wouldn't be necessary, and that if Cass would be good enough to keep an eye on her until she got home, she would pick her up when she got back to Riddle.

"Big surprise there," Cass muttered as she hung up the phone and returned it to her pocket.

Matthew and Lily were sitting in the kitchen reviewing what Lily had missed at school that day, so Cass decided to go sit on the front porch to await the pizza delivery guy. But more than that— she had someone else she wanted to talk to without Lily or Matthew listening in.

Green seemed to know her intentions. He was sitting on the porch railing, his leg swinging, as he had on Saturday. They watched each other quietly for a moment.

"You really did know me," Cass said at last. "From the time I was little. You were my first friend."

"You're the one who called me Green," the fae said in agreement. "I thought it was a little on the nose, but Alexandra explained that two-year-old humans have a bit of a limited vocabulary."

"Why didn't you tell me?" Cass asked.

Green looked at her derisively. "You wouldn't have listened. You weren't listening to the things I *was* saying."

"I'm sorry," Cass said. She sighed, leaning against the balustrade. "I can't believe I forgot."

"Time does funny things to the human mind. I've seen it, over the years. Old Mrs. Porter, she could remember the history of the woods to recite to anyone who would listen, but she couldn't remember her own name near the end. And when you *want* to forget—something that's painful, for example—your aunt said she thought you might have put up a block. Because of what happened to your other human."

"Jeremy?"

Green nodded. "Your Matthew is better."

Cass sighed again. "I know."

"I like him."

"I know that, too."

Green harrumphed. "If you know all this, then why aren't you doing something about it?"

"I will."

The fae grinned pointedly at her. "Is that a promise?"

Cass rolled her eyes. "I should know better than to make a promise in front of a fae now," she said. "But yes. That's a promise."

Green nodded, seeming satisfied. With a glimmer of light, he disappeared into the trees.

About an hour later, Mrs. Kowalski arrived to collect Lily. She'd already finished her pizza, but she still grumbled when her mother arrived.

"It's getting late anyway, kiddo," Matthew reminded her as they walked her to the door. "You still have school tomorrow."

"Seriously?" Lily groaned.

"Seriously. If I have to be there, you do too."

"Hey, you slept most of the day," Cass pointed out. "You should be plenty well-rested."

Lily stuck her tongue out at Cass but obliged. Cass's heart went out to the girl, though, at the sound of her mother's scolds on the way to the car. "You practically worried your father to death," she heard her say just before the car door slammed. She flinched, hoping Lily wouldn't take too much of the blame for her father's "respiratory distress." She might have to give Mr. Kowalski a word about that—after she informed him that she would not be selling her property to him after all. Maybe she could ask Green to give her some backup, since he could apparently show himself to humans at will.

"I should probably get going, too," Matthew said when they'd gone.

"Wait," Cass said. "First I need to talk to you."

Matthew winced. "About Saturday?"

Cass nodded. "About Saturday."

They went out to the porch, sitting on the wooden bench.

"Matthew, I want to apologize for the way I acted," Cass said, her stomach twisting in knots that were all nerves. For once, her premonitory jitters seemed to have settled. "I was out of line. I was... scared."

"Scared?" Matthew said. "Why should you be scared?"

Cass sighed. "Because of my... ability."

"Your faery blessing?"

She swallowed and nodded. "Maybe it's not as bad as Laney's. But to me it is." She explained to him about her premonitions; how sometimes they were stronger than others. And she explained to him about Jeremy.

"Cass," Matthew said quietly when she was finished. "I'm so sorry that happened to you. But you have to know, I'm not like him."

"I know you're not," Cass said, looking down at the peeling paint on the floor of the porch. "I was just afraid. Afraid of hurting you. But... more afraid of hurting myself. And I know that was selfish of me. I know there's probably nothing I can say to make up for that. I understand if you don't want to see me again. I just... I just wanted to be honest with you. For once."

Matthew was quiet for a moment. Then, to her surprise, he shifted to face her, taking her hand in his.

"Remember what I told you before? About the feelings I get?"

Cass nodded. "*Your* faery blessing."

Matthew smiled. "Right. Well, whatever it is... I've never felt more strongly than I do right now. Where I belong is right here next to you."

Cass's heart caught in her throat.

He ran his thumb over the back of her hand, making her skin tingle. "But if we're going to do this, we have to be honest."

Cass nodded. "I know. No more running. No more secrets."

Matthew grinned. "Promise? And I know now that you can't break promises when there are fae watching."

Cass laughed. "Promise."

He leaned over and kissed her, and she kissed him back. And this time she didn't run away. There'd be no more running.

An eternity later, Matthew finally said he needed to leave—he had school in the morning, Cass had to be at the library, and Tucker was probably driving the neighbors insane. It was close to midnight as she watched him drive away, but she didn't feel like sleeping. She felt like floating on a cloud.

Onyx strolled up to her, rubbing himself around her ankles as she closed the front door. "What are you angling for? Second dinner?" Cass asked, crouching to scratch him behind the ears. But to her surprise, when she straightened, the cat didn't head for the kitchen. Instead, he trotted to the stairs, stopping halfway up to look at her over his shoulder.

As she climbed the stairs after him, she heard a noise. A creaking, like a door swinging open after years of disuse. Her skin prickled.

She crept down the hallway, following the sound. At the end of the hall opposite the servants' staircase, the second-floor door to the observatory tower stood open, a square of light from within reflecting off the polished wood floor. Onyx sat in the square for a moment, watching Cass, before disappearing inside.

"Hello?" Cass called out. The only answer was a rustling sound, like the swish of skirts, or maybe the shuffling of papers.

She stepped inside, peeking around. The room was cluttered. On a table in the center of the bay window of the turret, a table lamp with a Tiffany glass shade glowed. She approached the table cautiously.

Beside the lamp was a small box, old and worn with a decorative lock on its front. Spread out face-down like a fan in front of this was a deck of tarot cards, crisp and new-looking. The pattern on their back matched the pattern on the cards Cass had been finding around the house ever since she arrived in Riddle. Only one card was face-up, placed in the center with the fanned cards around it. Cass picked it up, looking at it more closely. The illustration showed a wheel like a sundial floating in the clouds. A sphinx sat atop it, and four winged creatures flew around it. The caption read *Wheel of Fortune.*

She set the card down and turned her attention to the box. It was heavy when she lifted it, but wouldn't open when she tried the lid. It was locked. She turned it this way and that, but there was no sign of a key.

"*Your necklace,*" a voice whispered in her ear. Cass gasped, whirling around, but there was no one there but Onyx, batting at a spiderweb in the corner with one paw. And she knew the voice hadn't come from the cat. She *recognized* that voice.

"Aunt Alexandra?" she asked aloud. No answer came.

She set the box down and reached into her pocket, withdrawing the iron key. It slipped into the lock, and when she turned it, with a soft click the lid popped open.

Inside was a stack of papers, and on top of the stack was a note. Cass recognized the handwriting as Alexandra's. It read:

My darling Cassie,

I'm sorry to have left you with this burden on your own. I wish I could have helped you more, but if there's one thing I Saw clearly, it's that you could only arrive at this place on your own two feet. It was a riddle you had to solve on your own.

I'm so proud of the woman you've become, and I know that you will continue to grow throughout your life. May this be a blessing to you now on your journey.

Alexandra

Cass set the letter aside and began to rummage through the rest of the papers in the box. Stock certificates, certificates of deposit, and information on how to access them. There was enough in here to leave Cass financially secure for the rest of her life. She could fix up the house and maintain it in perpetuity.

Cass's eyes burned and she squeezed them closed. She understood why Alexandra had kept this away from her. If she'd known about this before—even just this morning—she would have taken the money and run. Alexandra had known that Cass needed to accept her role as caretaker on her own terms, and then she'd be provided for.

It was a riddle you had to solve on your own.

Cass put her necklace back around her neck and wrapped her fingers around the key. "Thank you, Aunt Alexandra," Cass whispered.

A gentle breeze ruffled the papers in the box and the cards on the table. Then it was gone.

Epilogue

One year later...

Cass stirred in her sleep, her eyes fluttering open as she felt Matthew's lips brush against hers. She looked around. The room was dark, and Matthew lay beside her atop the eyelet coverlet of their bed. He was re-reading *The Lion, The Witch and The Wardrobe* for probably about the tenth time in the last year. Onyx was sitting on the windowsill, his tail flicking as he gazed out into the shadows. From the floor near the fireplace, she could hear the sound of Tucker chewing on something in his crate—maybe a rawhide, or maybe his own foot, knowing that dog.

"Hey, sleepyhead," Matthew said cheerfully as she sat up, wiping the sleep from her eyes.

"What time is it?" she murmured.

"It's only about ten. You dozed off after dinner."

She remembered now. She'd just meant to lie down for a

moment, but she was exhausted. She and Matthew had spent the day painting downstairs, and they'd only gotten two rooms done.

She snuggled against his chest and he wrapped his left arm around her. His hand brushed the small of her back where her shirt had slid up slightly, his wedding band cool against her skin. They'd married less than a month before at a small ceremony in Foreston, at the Paine Estate. Matthew's sister Laney had been eager to plan the event, and Taryn got them a great discount on the caterer through her hotel contacts. Though they'd only known each other a short while, Cass found she quite liked her new sisters-in-law. They were more like Matthew than he was willing to admit.

There'd been no time for a honeymoon, what with school about to start, so after a brief stay in Washington they'd come back to Riddle, to their cheerful purple Victorian in the woods. It still needed a lot of work to be their dream home, but with the brownies and household elves helping out—when they felt like it—they'd made plenty of headway.

They still needed that air conditioner, though. Hopefully by next summer.

It was hard to believe how much had changed in a year's time, but the biggest change seemed to be Cass herself. She'd found settling into the role of caretaker to be far less strenuous than she'd feared. Maybe that was because she was finally willing to open up and let others in. With Matthew, Lily, and Darcy here, Emma just a phone call away, and even Green with his mischievous good will to support her, Cass was slowly learning to trust and to let go of the fears that had built up in her heart over a lifetime.

Still need to work on that whole antisocial thing, though, she thought wryly.

The one person who *wasn't* around was Tom Kowalski. After he returned from the hospital, Cass had gone to speak with him as planned. He was less than enthused about letting her out of their verbal agreement, but after some *persuasion* from Green, he'd come around. In fact, he suddenly felt the urge to spend more time working at his Portland-area investment company. After the meeting he'd been inclined to sell his Riddle home altogether, but the school counselor had urged the family not to uproot, insisting that Lily needed stability after her "runaway" incident. So Lily and her mother remained behind, and Mrs. Kowalski pledged to become a more attentive parent. Lily may have chafed over her mother's sudden switch from indifference to helicopter parenting, but Cass knew deep down that in a few years' time, she'd appreciate a stronger relationship with at least one of her parents.

And she always had the woods to escape to—more often than not with her new best friend Amelia Reynolds in tow. Though Cass was still hesitant, Lily had gone through with sharing her secret with Amelia; and Amelia, like Emma before her, had been more than understanding. The girls loved playing in the woods together, Lily relaying the hijinks of the fae to her friend. They promised to stay away from the warren, though. Even with the fae's alliance with the humans renewed by Cass's pledge to be the new Chatelaine, it was still better safe than sorry.

"Taryn called while you were asleep," Matthew said, setting his book aside.

"Yeah?" Cass said, shifting to look up at him.

"She wants to know if we can head out to Kings Valley next weekend. Said there's something that she needs your help with."

Cass furrowed her brows. "My help?"

He nodded. "She didn't get into it too much on the phone. She said she'd tell us more in person. But if it's your help she needs, I'm sure you know what that means."

Matthew's youngest sister had worked in the hospitality business for a few years, dreaming of saving up to open her own bed-and-breakfast. But by a stroke of good luck, over the summer she'd entered one of those contests Cass had seen in the news, to win a bed-and-breakfast through a writing contest, and right around the time of Cass and Matthew's wedding she learned that she'd won: a country inn in Kings Valley, a tiny community outside Corvallis. It was a fixer-upper, but Taryn had been eager for the challenge.

But if now she needed *Cass's* help... there must be fae nearby.

There's no such thing as coincidences.

"How far is it from here?" Cass asked.

"About two and a half hours," said Matthew.

"Not too bad. Maybe she just wants to surprise us with a mini-honeymoon at her new inn before she opens it up to other guests," Cass suggested.

Matthew laughed. "We can always hope."

Cass wrapped her arm around his neck, drawing him against her. "In the meantime," she whispered, "there's no time like the present for a little honeymoon at home."

"I couldn't have put it better myself," Matthew said, pressing his lips against hers.

Author's Note

Riddle is a real town located in Douglas County, Oregon. Living in Oregon myself, I can't count the times I've passed the "Riddle, Next Exit" sign on the freeway and imagined what sort of magic might take place in a town with such a curious name. I hope the citizens of Riddle don't mind that I borrowed their hometown for the setting of my book!

I tried to keep the setting as true to life as possible, but due to plot constraints, there were some things I had to take liberties with. As one example, the Riddle Public Library closed due to lack of funding in April of 2017, and subsequently reopened in June with an all-volunteer staff—there are no paid librarians like Cass and Darcy. I hope readers will pardon this inaccuracy, as well as the myriad others that I'm sure *riddle* (sorry, I couldn't resist) this book. Please remember that this is a work of fiction, and that all the characters and situations are products of my own imagination.

If you would like to help support the real Riddle Library and ensure it remains open for future generations to enjoy, please visit their website at RiddleLibrary.org.

Acknowledgments

The first person I want to thank is someone I never met in person, a woman named Betty who owned a beautiful property that bordered my home. She fought to protect it, but unfortunately the fight was lost after she passed away. Though I only got to enjoy them for a few years, Betty's woods were every bit as magical as the woods in *Alexandra's Riddle*, and that magic changed my life. I wish I could have saved them. There's not a day that goes by that I don't miss them. I hope that they will at least live on in this book.

I also want to thank everyone who helped make this book a reality. Thank you to my cover designer, Najla Qamber; to my editor, Rose Anne Roper; to my assistant, Esther Hadassah, for keeping my business running while I'm offline so that I can write; to Melissa Storm, for all your advice and support, and for being the best mentor an author could ask for; and to Karen Teal, for helping me appease the faeries.

Thank you to my family for all your support and for everything you do for me.

And, of course, TBTG.

About the Author

Elisa Keyston is an author of sweet romance with hints of magic, intrigue, and suspense. She was the series lead for the first season of The Pioneer Brides of Rattlesnake Ridge, a shared-world historical romance series from Sweet Promise Press, and she's also the author of the Northwest Magic series from Crimson Fox Publishing, a sweet contemporary romance series with a touch of magic and mystery set in her home state of Oregon. She's a graduate of Sonoma State University with a degree in history, which inspired her love of historical fiction and modern stories set in historic places. When she's not writing, Elisa spends most of her time gardening, collecting gnomes and fairies for her backyard, and fawning over her furbabies. Visit Elisa online and sign up for her newsletter at elisakeyston.com.

Other Books by the Author

THE NORTHWEST MAGIC SERIES

Old Flames

Fool's Gold (coming soon)

THE PIONEER BRIDES OF RATTLESNAKE RIDGE

Arriving from Arkansas

Sailing from Scotland (coming soon)